REV~~IEW COPY~~

FOR LIMIT~~ED~~

MW01222512

A Haunting at Richelieu High

A Penny Dreadful Investigation

A Novel by Bob Berry

Category: FICTION / General
            FICTION / Ghost
            FICTION / Thrillers
ISBN13:   Hardcover 978-1-4500-8263-1
            Softcover 978-1-4500-8262-4
LOC: 2010905133
Pages: 105
Trim Size: 9 x 6
Rights: Bob Berry
Publisher: Xlibris
            1663 Liberty Drive, Suite 200
            Bloomington, IN 47403
            888-795-4274 ext. 7879
            610-915-0294
            www.xlibris.com

Dear Reviewer:

Enclosed is a copy of **A Haunting at Richelieu High** by **Bob Berry.** It would be highly appreciated if you could take the time to read through and review this book.

Reviews may be submitted to marketingservices@xlibris.com and should contain the following information:

Book Title
Author
Reviewer (name of publication / media)
Contact information of reviewer

You may also submit your reviews via fax at (610) 915-0294, or mail to:

Xlibris Corporation
c/o Marketing Services Department
1663 Liberty Drive, Suite 200
Bloomington, IN 47403
USA

For any other concerns, please call (888) 795-4274 ext. 7879.

Thank you.

Xlibris Corporation

Contact: **Marketing Services**
(888) 795-4274 x. 7879
MarketingServices@Xlibris.com

1663 Liberty Drive, Suite 200, Bloomington, IN 47403

68785 FOR IMMEDIATE RELEASE

Witness *A Haunting at Richelieu High: A Penny Dreadful Investigation*
New book tells a chilling tale of horror and adventure

Poughquag, NY – (Release Date TBD) – For KC Watson, the oddest, most awful thing in the whole wide world had to be the first day of school. But the arrival of a mysterious new girl Penelope Dredalus, piques her interest. Determined to figure her out, KC begins trailing her and discovers a bigger mystery to unravel. Readers can follow the exciting events as they unfold in *A Haunting at Richelieu High: A Penny Dreadful Investigation*, a novel by Bob Berry.

KC could never resist a good mystery—and new student Penelope Dredalus was exactly just that. Quiet and very serious, she had a secretive air about her. Luckily she was in most of KC's classes, which makes getting the dirt on her a whole lot easier. During lunch, KC and her friend Air observe Penelope while she is talking on a cell phone. Suddenly the phone explodes in a shower of sparks. A day after that incident, KC follows Penelope to the basement of north wing of the school where they experienced something more terrifying.

As KC begins to know more about Penelope and who she is, she realizes there is a bigger mystery at school that they need to solve. But can two teenagers stand a chance against a vengeful spirit? *A Haunting at Richelieu High: A Penny Dreadful Investigation* will keep readers engrossed from the very first page until the last. For more information on this thrilling book, log on to www.Xlibris.com.

About the Author
Bob Berry is an illustrator, and designer. For the last 15 years his main focus has been in the children's market, illustrating books featuring Sesame Street characters, Dora the Explorer and Disney Princesses. *A Haunting at Richelieu High: A Penny Dreadful Investigation* is Bob's first novel. He lives with his family and spunky schnauser in upstate New York. Go to www.bobberryillustration.com to see Bob's artwork.

A Haunting at Richelieu High: A Penny Dreadful Investigation * by Bob Berry

A Penny Dreadful Investigation
Publication Date: June 29, 2010
Trade Paperback; $15.99 ; 105 pages; 978-1-4500-8262-4
Trade Hardback; $24.99 ; 105 pages; 978-1-4500-8263-1

For more information, contact Xlibris at (888) 795-4274 or on the web at www.Xlibris.com.

A Haunting at Richelieu High

A 'Penny Dreadful' Investigation

A Haunting at Richelieu High

A Penny Dreadful Investigation

Written and illustrated by
Bob Berry

Library of Congress Control Number:		2010905133
ISBN:	Hardcover	978-1-4500-8263-1
	Softcover	978-1-4500-8262-4
	Ebook	978-1-4500-8264-8

To order additional copies of this book, contact:
Xlibris Corporation
1-888-795-4274
www.Xlibris.com
Orders@Xlibris.com
68785

CONTENTS

Acknowledgments

PENNY DREADFUL BOOKLETS were very inexpensive publications printed in Great Britain during the nineteenth century. These little booklets featured lurid stories of vampires, stories of ghosts, and tales of bloodthirsty madmen, in short, some very *gothic* reading. I'd like to thank my father, John G. Berry, for making me aware of the original "penny dreadful." So thanks, Dad. I appreciate the inspiration.

While I have written fiction most of my life, *A Haunting at Richelieu High: A Penny Dreadful Investigation* is my first novel. I've spent most of my adult life working as a commercial illustrator. Most of my work over the last few decades has been in the children's market, and working in that area was a natural segue to writing this book. Special thanks also goes out to my wife, Cindy, who saw that the children's market was where I should be working and that I should try my hand at writing. Cindy also read through the manuscript several times and gave me much-needed input and encouragement.

I also have to thank my children, Emma and Daniel, who patiently listened as I read the first two chapters aloud. When I was done reading, they wanted to have more, and that gave me a reason to keep writing. I will also thank Emma for proofreading the early chapters of this book. Both Emma and Daniel served as models for the Watson kids, so I thank them for that as well.

Thanks to my lifelong friend Joseph G. Barrett for many discussions on writing in general and in structuring the narrative of this book in particular.

I also have to acknowledge my story editor, Jean Sheff. I gave her a very rough manuscript, and she slogged through the tome, making some much-needed and insightful changes.

I should also thank Leia Albiar and Judith Cruz at Xlibris for their excellent copy editing.

Finally, I want to thank my mother, Annette Berry. I was lucky to inherit her artistic ability and her perseverance. It takes both to create an illustration and write a novel. Thanks, Mom.

Bob Berry
March 18, 2010
Poughquag, New York

Chapter 1

First Day

THE ODDEST, MOST awful thing in the whole wide world has to be the first day of school. Well, maybe next to having a cavity drilled by the dentist or getting a shot, it isn't that bad, but it's up there in the "worst things ever" department. I mean, it's like visiting some old aunt or uncle on a perfectly beautiful summer day. You know you should be outside, but here you are, stuck in the confines of some dull, hot, totally boring place; and there's no escape. At least not until you've had your cheeks pinched and you've been forced to eat some totally awful culinary concoction.

That pretty much describes my first day of ninth grade at Richelieu High School. It was warm and beautiful outside, and I was sitting in a stuffy classroom, on the lowest rung of the Richelieu academic and social food chain. But don't get me wrong; it wasn't all that bad. First of all, I was wearing some of the latest fall couture. Second, I got to see all my friends from last year. FYI, almost everyone in my school is "well off," so most of my friends spend the summers at sleep-away camp or on an endless string of exotic vacations. In my family, exotic summer vacations consist of dips in our backyard pool and endless summer studies to prepare us for the next school year.

Thankfully, summer was a dim memory, and there I was in Mr. Walters's homeroom, surveying the class. I've known most of my classmates since kindergarten. I'm friends with most of them, and a few are my very best friends. Margaret George was my best friend since nursery school, but at the end of eighth grade, there was a family tragedy, which forced her and her mom to move to California. I really can't give more detail than that. It's just too sad.

But on the bright side, my friend *Air* was right across the isle from me. Oh, I should explain that Air isn't his real name. His real name is Alonzo Ignatius Rodriguez, but we call him Air for short. It's an especially good nickname because not only does it use the initials of his name but it also describes his single most-identifiable feature. Since he was old enough to stand, he's been totally into skateboarding; and although he's not that good at it, we all started calling him Air in honor of his constant quest to get some—air, that is, on his skateboard.

Well, as I looked around the homeroom, I saw most of the usual faces. It's kind of weird how some of them had changed so much in a couple of short months, while others had hardly changed at all. I wondered if my classmates saw any change in me. I knew I've gotten taller over the summer, and my hair was a couple of shades lighter. I knew I've changed a bit. My mom would say that I've filled out. Did any of them see it? Who knows? Did any of them see anything? Everyone's face had that weird "first day of school" look. They were all still in summer mode, and the grim reality of the new semester hadn't quite sunk in.

The homeroom was still pretty noisy, and some stragglers were drifting in. They were mostly newbies, new kids from other schools. Some of them looked like they got up that morning ready for another carefree August day, to be suddenly (and magically) whisked away to September. Some were still in their shorts, with bare feet casually slipped into sneakers or flip-flops. Others looked as if they were going on a job interview or something. One new kid was even wearing a tie! Imagine, a tie!

A few more new kids filed in, and one girl really got my attention, she seemed . . . different . . . kind of detached from the others. I smiled to myself. She was a mystery, and I liked a good mystery.

Just the look her outfit could be a clue. I have friends who are skateboarders like Air and the preppy types like Margaret, my BFF who had moved away. I know kids who are into retro grunge and kids who are totally goth, but this girl was hard to define. At first, I would have said goth, but that wouldn't be totally accurate. There was none of the wild jewelry, black nail polish, or tattoos; instead, she wore a black dress that came to about the middle of her calf, black tights, and some really horrendous black oxford shoes. The top of her dress was buttoned right up to her small pointed chin. And her arms were covered right to the wrists. Above that pointed chin was a cute but kind of sad or serious mouth (no lip gloss!). Her nose was thin and straight, and her hair was black, almost like a raven's feather, with an iridescent sheen. A perfect curtain of black bangs framed her most amazing feature, her eyes. They were wide set with long black lashes beneath naturally thin and well-shaped eyebrows. Her eyes were a tawny gold, almost like the eyes of a lion or a tiger. Her skin was olive and looked as if it could be a rich tan if she ever got into the sun.

This girl was a genuine mystery, and I made up my mind to keep my eyes on her.

Oops, I almost forgot to introduce myself. My name is Katarina Cassandra Watson, but all my friends call me KC. I've had the nickname since kindergarten. I guess that calling me by my initials was easier than saying Katarina Cassandra, so the initials stuck.

Just then, Air nudged me. "KC," he said in a hoarse whisper, "check her." Air had noticed our mysterious new classmate.

"I did. She's really different, interesting," I replied.

"I guess, but I think she's kinda spooky."

Mr. Walters told everyone to take a seat. "Mr. Rodriguez," he said as people began to settle down, "please remove your chapeau."

"Huh?" replied Air.

"Your hat, Mr. Rodriguez, please remove the beanie."

A couple of kids laughed. Air looked embarrassed and gave Mr. Walters a goofy grin as he palmed the knitted beanie off his head. Air was a sweet guy and a good friend but not always that fast on the uptake.

"Sorry," he said.

Mr. Walters took attendance by calling out everyone's name. And I got my first vital bit of info on this strange new girl. Her name was Penelope Dredalus. *What kind of name is that?* I asked myself as I spelled out her last name phonetically in my notebook.

Homeroom droned on for another twenty minutes as Mr. Walters went on about—I'm actually not sure what he went on about. I do know that he gave out our locker assignments and printouts of our classes and wished us luck as we crowded out of the classroom. I scanned my classes to make sure I got everything I signed up for, which I did, and compared classes with Air before we went our separate ways.

Chapter 2

Lunch

THE BEAUTIFUL THING about the first day of school is that you can get away with a lot by just claiming that you were confused. It's perfectly reasonable because most students are confused—on the first day, that is. As I made my way through the halls, I was met with a constant stream of puzzled faces and eyes glazed over from information overload. "First day" syndrome if I'd ever seen it. I mean, face it; being back at school after nearly three months of aimless freedom was a shock that might take us a month to get over or cause a major zit breakout.

Well, I decided to use the relative confusion of the first day of school to follow my mysterious new classmate. I felt a little silly. I wasn't sure why she interested me so much. Maybe it was just a way to get through the first day, or maybe it was because she was so different from the other kids in my school. She had a somber quality about her that went way beyond the weird dark clothing. This girl had a story!

It turned out that the mysterious Penelope Dredalus was in most of my classes, which made getting the dirt on her a whole lot easier. She was *very* serious all the time and sat quietly and attentively took notes on whatever first-day info the teachers were giving out. I was taking notes too in between glances at my exotic classmate. Hey, that was it! She was exotic!

At fifth period lunch, I sat a couple of tables across from her. Air came bopping over a few minutes later, holding a lunch tray filled with a double serving of tacos, chips, and milk. He wasn't the biggest guy, but he sure could eat. His beanie was back on his head, and his usually sandy hair was peeking out from under it in dark, wet ringlets.

"Gym?" I asked.

"Yeah, gym, calisthenics, and twenty-five meter dashes for the whole period just to get us back into shape. At least that's what Coach Roudy Rollier says. I think he just likes to torture us!"

"Ms. Crawford, the girls' coach, I mean the 'women's phys ed instructor,' gives us the same hype. She says if we're not in shape by the end of summer vacation, we'll never be. I feel bad for the kids who spent the summer playing video games."

"Yeah," Air affirmed as he took a humongous bite out of a taco of questionable quality and origin.

"Hey," he said, "there's your mystery woman!"

I leaned in toward him. "I know. I've been studying her all day."

"You mean you've been *following* her all day."

"Well, she *is* in most of my classes."

"C'mon, KC. I know how nosy you are."

"*Nosy?* I just like a good mystery."

"Nosy!"

"MYSTERY!"

"Whatever." He threw up his hands.

I leaned even closer, glancing back over my shoulder. "And she sure is that, a mystery, I mean. She doesn't seem to know anybody and keeps pretty much to herself."

"Ooooo, mysterious."

I jabbed him in the ribs. "I know *that's* not particularly weird, but oh my gosh, *just look at her!*"

Air's head tilted to the side, and he screwed up his face a little. "I think she's kinda hot . . . in a nerdy, goth kind of way."

"HMMPH!" My back went rigid, and I abruptly folded my arms across my chest.

Air turned toward me with a really surprised look on his face. "What? What did I say?"

"Nothing." Just like a boy, clueless.

Honestly, I never thought of Air as anything but a friend, but suddenly I found myself getting jealous that he found this new girl "hot."

"Well, look there." He pointed. "Your friend Ms. Dreadfulus has some friends. See, she's on her cell."

"Dredalus," I corrected. "Her last name is Dredalus."

Air looked at me for a second as if he was processing my words. "Well," he said, "she's so gloomy that I think *Dreadfulus* or *Dreadful* fits her better."

I smiled and gave him a little shove.

I sat there quietly for a moment, watching our mysterious classmate. Air was oblivious as he munched on his taco.

"She's been on the cell for a while," I said.

"UGN," he grunted in agreement as he continued to eat.

"She's not looking too happy."

Air's interest was piqued. He swallowed a huge mouthful of taco with a loud *gulp*. He leaned forward. "She looks really upset, whoa!"

Just then, the cell phone she was holding gave off a shower of sparks, and it seemed to fly out of her hand. The phone arched across the cafeteria, and it hit some big sophomore right in the back. The sophomore was Brett Henry, who was just about the biggest and most obnoxious up-and-coming jock in school. He stood up like a bolt and whirled around, glaring.

"Who did that?"

Dead silence. All heads turned toward Brett Henry.

Penelope Dredalus stood up slowly and walked toward Brett. She stood there for a heartbeat looking up at him, her head barely even with his shoulders. "I'm sorry," she said in an even voice, her accent obvious. "My cell phone exploded. I did not mean for it to hit you."

Brett stood there, his chest heaving, still angry. He scanned the petrified crowd and then looked back at the smaller ninth-grade girl with the big golden eyes.

"'S okay, not a problem." He even managed a crooked little smile and bent down to retrieve the singed cell phone. She took the phone and turned around to go back to her seat.

"Who *are* you?" he asked.

"Penelope Dredalus. I am a new student this year." She turned away and walked quickly back to her seat. Brett stood there a minute and then sat down with his friends. Somebody said something, and they all laughed. The cafeteria got loud again.

I turned back to Air, who was sitting there with his jaw gaping. I reached over and pushed his mouth shut.

"Whoa, did you see that?"

"I saw it, Air, but I don't know *what* I saw. Look, she's got another cell phone."

Penelope had reached into her black leather backpack and pulled out another cell phone. She started to punch in a number but stopped and looked around the room. She jammed the phone back into her backpack and quickly left the cafeteria.

"Wow!" said Air. "How sweet is that? Two cells."

I tugged the sleeve of his jersey. "Let's follow her."

We both gathered our bags and books and pushed through the heavy cafeteria doors. The hallway was empty and quiet. She must have moved pretty quickly down one of the hallways that intersected in front of the cafeteria entrance. Air was chewing loudly on the remains of a taco; I motioned for him to keep quiet. Then we both heard a voice coming from the hallway leading to the main lobby. We walked toward the sound.

Now I could definitely hear Penelope's voice. She was speaking very quietly. We neared the corner of the hallway, and I inched my face ever so slightly forward. I caught a glimpse of Penelope hunched over her phone.

"Papa," she said, "I must leave here now. No, Papa, I can't tell you now. Please come and get me. I will tell them that I don't feel well. Yes, I will see you in fifteen minutes. Thank you, Papa."

I could see her fold the phone and quickly walk toward the school office.

"See, KC, no mystery. She's sick. And she calls her dad Papa. That's weird."

I just looked at Air. Like I said, *totally clueless*.

Chapter 3

Neighbors

WHEN THE SCHOOL bus dropped Air and me off at the corner of Whitney Street and Battle Avenue, I was exhausted. Air and I live a block away from each other. He seemed to want to hang and talk, but after an exhausting first day, I just wanted to get home and chill. The first day of school always gives me a headache. Plus the September heat was a killer. I wish someone could explain to me why September *feels* hotter than August. I'm totally mystified. It's like the way a Sunday in the summer can feel like an eternity while a Sunday during the school year can be over in a blink of an eye. Just plain weird.

I said good-bye to Air and headed up Battle Avenue and dragged my backpack and myself up to the front porch of our small wood-frame house and checked the mailbox. Nothing but flyers and ads, which I left for Dad to bring in when he came home. No point in overtaxing myself.

"Mom, I'm home!" I yelled out as I came in the door.

"I'm in the kitchen, KC. So how was the first day of ninth grade?"

I rolled my eyes. Mom was making a big deal out of ninth grade as if it was my first day of college or something.

"'Kay."

Mom came out into the hallway, wiping her hands in a dishtowel.

"Come on, Katarina"—I hated it when she calls me that—"it had to be more than just '*kay*." Mom's imitation of my voice was way too close and a little aggravating.

"C'mon, Mom. It was school. It was okay. I got the classes I wanted, and Air's in most of them."

Mom placed a finger thoughtfully on her chin and looked up at some spot on the ceiling. "Well, I guess that's all right as long as Alonzo isn't too much of a distraction."

I blew out a long sigh, exasperated. "Mom, Air and I've been in practically the same class since grade school . . . He hasn't been a distraction *yet!*"

"You're both teenagers now, and things change so much at your age."

I cringed a little, knowing that she was getting ready to give me one of her famous lectures about the challenges of adolescence. I decided to try a diversionary tactic.

"We have a really interesting new girl in school. I think she's Greek or something."

"That's nice. Now as I was about to say—"

"Her cell phone exploded today!"

"Exploded! I didn't think that was possible."

"Really, Mom. Her cell exploded right in the cafeteria. There was a big shower of sparks. The phone flew right out of her hand and hit Brett Henry right in the back. Boy was he mad. You should've seen him!"

"KC . . ."

"Yes, Mom?"

"I know what you're doing." She folded her arms across her chest.

"I'm sorry, Mom, but I'm tired. And I'm really not in the mood for a lecture."

She put her hand up to my cheek. "Okay, sweetie, I'll let you off this time, but please don't let Air distract you. Friends are good, and you'll have plenty, but remember—"

"I know," I said. "My education is the most important thing."

"Exactly!"

I chilled for a while, had a snack, and listened to my little dweeb brother, James, go on about his adventures in fourth grade. I have a very low tolerance for booger jokes and milk shooting out of people's noses, so while my mother was enthralled, I quietly slipped out of the kitchen and up the stairs to my room.

My room wasn't huge, but it was mine, and I loved it. I dropped my backpack down near the closet and threw myself onto the bed.

After dinner, Air called me to ask me about math homework. Imagine, homework on the first day! Well, that was Mr. Gagliardo. We called him *the Gag* because the huge amounts of homework he gave would make your stomach turn. This year, he wasn't wasting anytime. Math was my worst subject, and I had a bad feeling about being in his class. Air was feeling the heat too. We tried to work out the homework over the phone and decided that it might be best to wait until tomorrow.

"Hey," I said, "before you hang up, I forgot to mention that I saw Penelope get picked up."

"Yeah?"

"Yeah, and you should've seen the car . . . big black Benz. It looked like an old one, like a classic or something. I couldn't see who was driving it, but she must have been watching from the lobby 'cause the second it pulled up, she was in the car, and it drove away."

Of course, all the importance of these subtle observations were lost on Air. There was just dead silence for a minute, then he said that he had to go feed his iguana, Don. That was a big joke to Air, but I never really got it.

I hung up the phone and fell back on my bed. It was about seven o'clock but still light outside, so I thought I'd give my dog, Frisket, a walk. We lived on Battle Avenue. I never understood why it was called Battle Avenue until I was old enough to go out on my own, and I discovered a sweet little playground and monument dedicated to the battle that was fought here during the Revolutionary War—duh—so hence the name Battle Avenue. The neighborhood was called Battle Hill, and a lot of the local streets had patriotic names like Independence, Liberty, and Concord.

The section of Battle Hill I lived in was a short walk from downtown White Plains. Most of the houses around here were pretty grand in their day. Some had big columns like that of Greek or Roman temples and terraced yards that led down to the street. Others were like Spanish haciendas with wrought iron gates, stucco walls, and roofs of overlapping terra-cotta tiles. The grandest and weirdest of these houses was at the corner of Whitney Street and Battle Avenue. It was a huge monstrosity, three levels high, styled to look like a rustic Italian villa. The angled roof was covered in red terra-cotta tiles, and the thick walls were made of peach-colored stucco. Everything about the house made it look more like a fortress than a home. Whoever built the place really liked their privacy! The house had one of the biggest yards in the neighborhood, enclosed by an ornate iron fence. About every twelve feet or so, the fence was anchored by tall red brick pillars. The front gate of the house was actually on Whitney. It was decorated with swirls and leaf shapes, all cleverly made in wrought iron. A wide flagstone walk connected the front gate to the main entrance of the house, which was a huge oak door protected by a deep portico guarded by four huge Corinthian columns (I remember that from art history). Over the ground-level porch was a second smaller porch also nestled behind the same four big columns. The weirdest feature was a small porch that rested on top of the four columns and went back into the main roof in the form of a dormer. This small third-floor porch was repeated on all four corners of the red-tiled roof. The whole effect was odd. To add to the mystery, it

Everything about the house made it look more like a fortress than a home.

had been abandoned for years. I always liked to walk past it and imagine what it must be like inside.

As I came down the sidewalk, I crossed Whitney Street to take Frisket into the small park. This put me directly across the driveway of the big house. The ornate gate was closed as usual, but now there was a car there. My jaw dropped as I moved in for a better look. The car was the same car that had picked up Penelope Dredalus at school.

"Come on, Frisket," I said. "We've really got to get home and call Air . . . He won't believe THIS!" Frisket gave me one sad, soulful look then bounded alongside me up Battle Avenue.

BOB BERRY

Chapter 4

Day Two

I COULDN'T WAIT to get up and get to school the next day. I was getting obsessed with this mysterious new neighbor who lived only five doors from my house. I made the mistake of sharing this with Air on the bus, and he told me as much. I sat in a huff the rest of the way to school. When we got off in front of Richelieu, I tossed my backpack over one shoulder and walked quickly off. I guess Air was more in tune than I give him credit for; he came running up to me, his big baggy jeans rustling.

"KC, wait up. Listen, I've known you since second grade. I'm not dissing you. I just don't think it's too healthy to get all focused on this new girl. If there's anything weird going on, we'll find out soon enough . . . Meanwhile, just go easy."

I looked at Air as if I'd never seen him before. He was actually making a lot of sense.

I gave him a friendly punch in the arm and smiled at him. "You're right. I should just lighten up. See you in homeroom."

Before I knew what I was doing, I gave him a little kiss on his cheek, and I was so embarrassed that I practically ran to my locker. I fished out the books for my morning classes and checked my class schedule one more time.

By the time I reached Mr. Walters's homeroom, the last bell rang. I found a seat and looked around the class. Air was a couple of seats in front of me, hunched way over, drawing something in his notebook. Mr. Walters came into the room, tapped Jeleal Murphy on the shoulder, and motioned for him to remove the earbuds and put the MP3 player away. Of course, he reminded Air to remove his beanie. Air glanced back at me with a goofy smile. I quickly looked down. I could feel my cheeks flush. I shouldn't have kissed him. Boys can be so weird about a simple kiss on the cheek.

I scrunched down into my seat and waited for morning announcements. The public address droned on about upcoming stuff like pep rallies and openings in the editorial staff for the junior yearbook. The whole school thing was coming at me way too fast. I groaned to myself and caught my head in my hands. Just then, Penelope Dredalus walked into class. She was fifteen minutes late. I caught her out of the corner of my eye as she walked up to Mr. Walters's desk and handed him a note. Today the frumpy black dress was gone, replaced by knitted, short-sleeved, turtleneck black sweater and black jeans of some velvety material. A thick black belt hung at her waist, and instead of the frumpy oxford shoes, she wore soft black leather boots with a very low heel and thin sole. She barely made a sound as she padded past my desk. I couldn't help noticing a few of the boys (Air included!) turning their heads to get a better look as she went to her seat. Well, I have to admit, she did look cute in a dark and mysterious way. Maybe *severe* would be a better word. Her black mane was pulled into a tight bun at the back of her head, and perched on top of her head was an odd pair of sunglasses. They weren't exactly stylish; in fact, they were clunky with smoky lenses and a really thick nerdy black frame.

Before she could see me looking at her, I turned around to face the front of the room. Air was looking at me with a knowing look; he nodded toward Penelope's direction.

"See," I mouthed so he could read my lips. He nodded and turned around.

The homeroom bell sounded over the intercom, and everybody rushed out of homeroom to get to their next class. Air joined me in the crowded hallway.

"Did you see that?"

Suddenly I was feeling mad at Air again. "Did I see *what*, Mr. Rodriguez?" I said coldly.

"Your friend *Penny Dreadful*."

"Who?"

"*Penny Dreadful*, that's what all the guys are calling her."

"Her name is Dredalus," I said. "It's Greek!"

"Well, whatever it is, she's hot . . . in a penny dreadful sort of way!"

"And you boys like *that*?!"

"Well, duh . . . Yeah. She's got that whole Lara Croft slash Catwoman thing going on. Big improvement over yesterday."

I was fuming! If I stayed with him another minute, I would have done something I'd regret. I stormed off.

As I power walked down the hall, I flashed a quick look over my shoulder at Air. There he was in the middle of first-period hall traffic, looking lost and bewildered.

Truth was, this new girl was starting to get under my skin too, but in a different way. I guess that as you start to become a teenager, you start to see all the funny little ironies that life can throw you. Suddenly the demure nerdy *new girl* was on every boy's "must see" list. It was only the second day of school, and I wasn't ready for all this drama.

My next class was PE, which I was in *absolutely* no mood for. I stormed into the girls' locker room to find (who else) but Penelope Dredalus jogging past in full gym uniform. She was in my PE class! I went to a locker and changed quickly, but by the time I got out to the gym floor, everyone was standing in two neat rows in front of the somewhat scary Ms. Crawford.

She blew a sharp, piercing note on her whistle, and all the girls kind of came to attention.

"Good to see you finally joined us, Ms. Watson."

"Sorry, Coach."

"PE starts at 8:40 sharp girls . . . Let's keep that in mind, please."

The next forty minutes were a mixture of stretching and strength exercises, calisthenics, and jogging four times around the quarter-mile-long track, which was next to the football field. Ms. Crawford believed that what didn't kill you would only make you stronger or something like that. Most of us felt like dying after her first class. Exhausted, we were shuffling back into the gym and on to the relief of the showers. I saw Ms. Crawford standing by the gymnastic equipment. There on the balance beam, Penelope Dredalus was performing this amazing series of handsprings. On her last one, she tucked herself into a ball and landed perfectly on the mat. Ms. Crawford was clapping wildly as she called us over.

"Girls, girls, before you go to the showers, I'd like you all to come over here and meet someone," she said.

We all groaned under our breath but marched dutifully across the gym to join our PE teacher.

"Girls, we are so lucky to have Ms. Penelope Dredalus in our school. Two years ago, she was living in Czechoslovakia. There, she was in accelerated gymnastics program training for the 2008 Olympics in Beijing. She was preparing for the rhythmic and artistic portions of the program, and I also understand that she was a dark horse in the fencing competition as well."

Penelope just stood there, rocking on her feet, hands clasped behind her, obviously uncomfortable with the spotlight.

The rest of the class did little to encourage her. They stood stone-faced. There were a couple of giggles and some muffled comments.

"Well," continued Ms. Crawford "I just wanted to make you all aware that Richelieu will be starting a competitive gymnastics program this year, and we were hoping to attract Ms. Dredalus and anyone else who wishes to try out. Okay, ladies, to the showers."

As I walked away, I overheard Penelope say to our PE teacher, "Thank you, Ms. Crawford. I will first have to talk to my father for permission to try out."

"Hopefully, he will say yes."

"I will let you know as soon as I am able, but now I must go to my next class."

If Ms. Crawford said anything in reply, I didn't hear her. A heartbeat later, Dredalus was bounding past me into the locker room. After that, I lost her in the confusion of thirty girls rushing to get to their next class.

I barely made it to second-period math. Air was there, sitting toward the back of the class. I sat a few seats in front of him. I wasn't so mad at him anymore. I guess I worked off some steam at PE, but I wasn't going to let him know that. Mr. Gagliardo started to hit us with several "simple" algebraic equations. Of course, we all sat there dumbfounded. Frustrated, he started to go over some of the basics, trying to help us to understand exactly *why* we needed algebra in the first place. Most of us were lost as we left his class forty minutes later. The Gag just watched us file out, shaking his head. Third and fourth period went okay but a little confusing. Spanish and English back-to-back could really tax a young mind. I looked forward to lunch and a peaceful study hall during sixth period.

This was the best kind of study hall because it was assigned to the upstairs library. Richelieu High was built back in the 1930s, and it was a really cool school, like something out of the movies. All brick with big arched windows, granite-floored hallways, and interior paneling so rich with history that you could practically smell it. The upstairs library was especially cool. From the heavily varnished floors to the transoms over its wide entrance doors, it was classic. The library was a big room that always seemed to absorb all sound. Maybe it was the book-lined walls or the six freestanding bookshelves that dominated the center of the room, but it always seemed like a dark, silent cavern. Even the huge bank of

. . . she tucked herself into a ball and landed perfectly on the mat.

tall windows couldn't usher in enough light to brighten up the room. Scattered throughout the library were fifteen heavy oak tables and matching chairs where students could read or study. There were several prehistoric workstations hidden in the darker recesses of the library where students could access the library's database.

The librarian, Mrs. Woods, had a commanding view of the library from behind the bulky circulation desk that was positioned in the huge room, between the two tall entrance doors. She had been at Richelieu when my parents went to the school back in the late seventies. According to my dad, time had not changed Mrs. Woods. She dressed the same, had the same hairstyle, and ran the same very tight operation.

I was just getting out my MP3 player, looking forward to forty minutes of rest, when through the door, I spied Ms. Dreadful back in her slinky black outfit, walking at a fast clip. Suddenly the mystery was on again. She looked as if she was trying her hardest not to break into a run, and she had a very serious expression on her face.

Okay, I admit it: I'm *impulsive*. I sprang up and asked the student librarian for a restroom pass and was quickly following the girl in black through the north wing of the school. She didn't make a sound in those soft leather boots, and I did my best to keep quiet in my flip-flops. Fortunately, there were lots of cubbies and connecting halls for me to duck into, so I could follow her from a distance. At the end of the north wing, she went down a stairwell, descending past the ground floor. She was headed for the basement, and she was in a real hurry. I followed quietly, sliding down the handrail until I stopped at the basement. Off to the south of the building were the shop classes. The north end was mainly utility rooms and additional banks of unused lockers and some big room that some of the kids said used to be a swimming pool or a bowling alley.

The stairwell emptied into an alcove set back from the hallway. I was able to carefully peer around the corner into the dark corridor. She was standing dead still in the middle of the gloomy hall. Slowly she began looking in all directions. She was constantly pulling the dark glasses down over her eyes, then returning them to their perch on top of her head. She seemed to be looking for *something. But why sunglasses?* I asked myself. In this light, she wouldn't be able to see a thing. Then she reached into her back pocket and pulled out what looked a little like a cell phone, but it had some funny multicolored screen on the face of it, and she kept passing it back and forth. As she was swinging around toward my direction, she froze. I ducked back into the alcove, pushing my back into the wall, hoping

BOB BERRY

After a few seconds, with my heart hammering in my ears, Penelope Dredalus came into view.

that she hadn't seen me. She wasn't making a sound, but I had a feeling she was coming toward me, so I inched further into the dark corner of the stairwell. I managed to get myself partially behind a big standpipe, and I waited, barely breathing. After a few seconds, with my heart hammering in my ears, Penelope Dredalus came into view. She was still sweeping the device in an arc in front of her, and occasionally, she would point it up toward the ceiling. The sunglasses were down over her eyes. Right at the opening of the stairwell, she paused again.

I started to feel a pressure in my ears, like the feeling you get when you're in a plane or driving up a mountain. Added to the pressure in my ears was a rushing sound coming from all around me. It was as if the entire space of the long dark hallway was gasping for air. The pressure started to build and build, and I clasped my hands over my ears and shut my eyes tight. Then nothing. I squinted one eye open, and Penelope was still standing there, motionless. Then there was another change in the air. It became dank and cold. The hair on my neck started to stand up and goose bumps sprouted all over my arms. I wanted to run, but I couldn't. Somewhere from the deep blackness of the hallway, I started to hear this hard metallic crash that was moving toward us like the sound of an old freight train heard from a great distance. The sound built up and up on itself, then there was a sound like a loud explosion. I opened my eyes in terror. For a brief second, I saw every locker in the hallway opening and slamming itself shut in succession. It was like a wave of clashing metal doors and earsplitting sound.

Before I could react, Penelope was on me and had me by the arm.

Chapter 5

Pranked

"YOU!" SHE SAID as she grabbed my arm in a powerful grip. "We have got to go NOW!"

We scrambled up the stairwell, the sound reverberating all around us. We stumbled, and I skinned my shins twice, but she never let go of my arm. When we finally reached the light and air of the ground floor, I could see teachers and students poking their heads out of the classrooms. Penelope turned toward me, and with a little smirk, she said in her accented voice, "It looks like everyone else heard it too."

Mr. Cortez, the principal, was the first to reach us.

"Are you girls all right? What was that?" We shrugged our shoulders.

"We don't know," said Penelope, glaring at me briefly. I was sure she was telling me to keep quiet, so I did.

He looked down at my bleeding shins. "You'd better go to the nurse's office. We haven't moved it downstairs yet." He looked at Penelope. "Can you go with her, please?" I was glad not to have to go down there again.

Mr. Foote, the maintenance man, was quickly at his side with a flashlight, and then they were bounding down the stairs toward the fading echo.

Once we were out of earshot of the teachers and students gathered around the north stairwell, I whirled around and grabbed Penelope by the arm.

"Okay," I said, "what just happened?"

She stepped around me and kept walking. I followed her, my shins hurting at every step. Again, I was met with that odd little smirk and the Eastern European accent. "What do you think happened?"

"Well, I don't know, but I'm scared half out of my wits, and I'm bleeding."

"You are bleeding because you wear shoes better suited for the seashore . . . Your flip-flops caused you to fall *up* the stairs while you were running away."

"Yeah, but *what* was I running away *from*?"

She shrugged her shoulders. "I'd say that you were running away from a bunch of lockers slamming themselves shut."

Exasperated, I grabbed her by the arm again. I got right up in her face, staring into those tawny eyes. "And exactly *how* did that happen?"

She smiled back. "That seems to be the question on everyone's mind. Here is the nurse. I have to get to a class . . . Ciao." And she smiled and padded away into the gathering crowd of students.

Long story short: the school nurse put some foul orange stuff on my shins, bandaged them up, and called my mom. She arrived in twenty minutes, and we drove home. Well, that's one way to get out of school. She had me sit in the family room. And she turned on some lame daytime soap. But she did bring me a cool glass of milk and some chocolate chip cookies. Mom sat down on the couch beside me. She was confused, and I really couldn't help her much. I was still pretty confused myself.

"One more time," she said, "what exactly happened?"

"Mom, all I know is that there was a loud bang all over school like a bunch of lockers slamming all at once, and I got scared, and I skinned my shins falling up the stairs."

"Does anyone know what caused this bang?"

"Nope."

"Everything seemed normal enough when I got there," she said.

"Yup." I was in monosyllable mode.

"Maybe the furnace backfired."

"Maybe."

"Or maybe it was a prank."

"Yup," I said, relishing the cookies and milk. "Maybe it was all just a prank."

As I munched on my cookies, all I could think of was that Penelope Dredalus and I would be discussing this *real soon*.

*   *   *

That same afternoon, Air dropped by. He came to the front door asking for me. News travels fast in our school, and I had a feeling that he might come over to see how I was, so I asked Mom to tell him that I was resting. I really didn't want to see him. I decided to let him stew for a while. Honestly, I don't think I like Air in a romantic way, but him noticing Penelope really got me mad—no, jealous. She was no prettier than me, but she was an "exotic." Maybe that was it. I looked at myself in the mirror and

      BOB BERRY

tried on a couple of different sunglasses. I piled my hair up on top of my head in a rough mock-up of a sophisticated style. I dropped my hands to my side in disgust. It was hard to look exotic when you had sun-streaked auburn hair and remnants of childhood freckles sprinkling your nose. I sat down at my laptop and opened up the browser. Maybe there were some answers on the Internet.

Chapter 6

More Questions than Answers

I SAT AT my computer until my eyes felt as if they were going to fall out of my head. Mom had popped into my room, first cajoling then demanding that I go to sleep. Eventually, she just gave up and went to bed. My dad knew better than to get involved in bedtime issues. I'd *always* been a night owl.

My research was getting me nowhere. I went back and forth between searching the Web for inexpensive makeovers, hairstyles, and accessories to weird psychic stuff. The events of the day were still swirling around in my head. There were tons of sites devoted to the unusual and the paranormal. The explanations ran the spectrum from earth tremors to bad wiring to aliens living among us. The hardest part was that I wasn't exactly sure what had happened. I remembered the weird rise in air pressure and drop in temperature. And then the whole bank of lockers *opening* and *shutting* themselves with tremendous force. Maybe earth tremors weren't that far off.

It was almost midnight, and I was just getting ready to shut down when I heard the ping of an instant message. I went to my mail and opened it. It was from amphoragirl96@ironwoodmuseumofantiquities.edu. I rubbed my eyes. I didn't remember any amphoragirl96, and I certainly never heard of Ironwood Museum of Antiquities. But as I read the message, the source of this strange IM became quite clear.

KC,

    aftR our adventure 2day, I knO ther R lots of :-Qz n yor mind. We hav 2 MEt 2moro & TLK prv8lE

[After our adventure today, I know there are lots of questions in your mind. We have to meet tomorrow and talk privately.]

P.

Penelope! How did she get my e-mail address? The cursor sat there blinking at me, waiting for me to reply. On one hand, I thought that it would probably be better just to tell her I wasn't interested, that I didn't need to know what happened today. But that, of course, would be totally bogus. I was dying to know, or at least find out what *she* thought had happened. I took a deep breath and replied.

P,

   2moro 5th period study hall, I'll sgn us ^ 4 a prv8 study r%m off d library. swNd gud?
   [Tomorrow, fifth period, study hall. I'll sign us up for a private study room off the library. Sound good?]

KC

The instant messaging beeped a reply.

:)

I fell back into my chair and groaned. "Great, now I'll never get to sleep."

I drifted off just about an hour before the alarm rang. Today would be a killer. Good thing it was the first Friday of the first week of school. I pulled myself out of bed like somebody escaping quicksand. Mom came in with a concerned look on her face.
"Up all night again, young lady?"
I held my head in my hands. "Busted."
"How are you going to get through school today?"
"It's Friday."
"You'll be falling asleep in class."
"I'll be okay . . . But look at the time. I've really got to bounce."
Mom gave me a funny look.
"I mean I've got to get going."
"Here, take this." She handed me a cup of really light coffee with a lot of sugar in my favorite old china cup. "This will get you going."
I gulped it down. "This will have me bouncing off the walls. Thanks!"

As predicted, I pretty much slogged through the morning, using whatever energy Mom's coffee gave me to stay awake. By fifth period, I was feeling as if I could just lean up against a wall and crash. But the prospect of having a private meeting with Ms. P woke me up.

I gathered up my Spanish books and speeded down the hallway, swerving in and out of oncoming student traffic, zipping in and out of little spaces left open by the less swift-footed. Just then, I saw the heavy library doors, and I bolted through the crowd.

"Hey! Watch it!"

"Sorry."

"Ouch, my foot!"

"Excuse me."

"Dude."

"Sorry."

I finally made it to the library doors and quickly slipped in. I was instantly overwhelmed by the silence of the library.

I went over to the student working at the desk and asked for a private study room. Luckily, there were a couple of study rooms available. I took the one farthest down the narrow hallway.

The study room was small with only a small work desk and two very uncomfortable-looking metal chairs. I fell heavily into the one near the far wall, exhausted.

I looked up just as Penelope thrust her head into the room. She was smiling, but she looked nervous. I managed to smile back at her. I was a little nervous too. I was a little shy around kids I didn't know, and she was a little—what's the word? *Intimidating*.

Penelope was obviously dressed for our first meeting, abandoning her usual all-black outfits for a white tailored shirt and a black skirt over black tights. She had on those atrocious school shoes again. She dropped her books with a thud and sat down. She sat there for a second, her back straight, hands placed carefully on her lap. She looked down at her hands then took a deep breath and turned to look at me.

"I wanted to see you about what happened yesterday." She had an odd smile on her face, her accent seemed heavier. "But I really do not know how to start."

I sat there for what seemed like a minute just looking at her, trying to understand what this strange girl was all about and what she wanted from me.

I leaned forward on my chair. "I went online and tried to see if I could find any similar type of events. Nada. I came up with nothing. But look, I printed out a load of stuff that could be related." I pulled out a thick pile of papers from my backpack.

"May I study those?" she said.

"Sure, knock yourself out," I said.

"Why would I want to do that?"

"No," I laughed. "I mean, yes, study them as much as you want . . . I really don't think they'll help much."

"You are probably correct."

I leaned in a little closer to her, thumbing to the page that I thought might give us the best explanation. "Here, look at this article. It's about convection currents in large buildings that could explain the pressure change that we felt."

"Perhaps."

"Or this one on *seismic activity*, you know, like earthquakes and stuff. Maybe it was something like that."

"Maybe."

She continued leafing through the printouts then stopped at several pages I had stapled together. She shuffled them to the front of the printouts.

She looked at me for a second as if she was sizing me up. "KC, I felt no tremors in the ground. Did you?"

"No, but it seemed like a logical explanation."

"And I would think that any convection currents would be a constant in a building. This was an unusual event, yes?"

"Well, yes, I mean, I guess so. It never happened before, at least not last year."

"You were following me, why?"

I looked down, a little embarrassed. "Well, face it. You're not the average, everyday ninth grader. I was curious about you. *And* there was that weirdness with the exploding phone in the cafeteria the first day of school."

"You saw that?"

"Penelope, everyone saw that. It was weird. Then I saw you slinking around the halls yesterday in your *ninja suit*. I figured you were up to something, so I followed you. *Which* reminds me, before the lockers slammed, you had another funny-looking cell phone you were waving around. What the heck was that? Did it cause what happened?"

"No, KC. It didn't. It was a device for detecting thermal and electromagnetic fields."

She leaned back in her chair, looking pained. Again, she looked at me with those strange tawny eyes. There was a serious expression, as if she was trying to read my mind.

"KC, we both had a rare privilege yesterday. We experienced something many people do not, but we need to talk further, and I don't think this is the place to do it."

"Why?"

"We might be overheard."

"By who?"

"Whom . . ."

"By whom . . . You mean like a hidden camera or something?"

"Or *something*, yes."

"This is whack!"

She reached out and took a hold of my arm. "KC, listen to me. I cannot explain what I think might be going on here, but I can tell you that my being here might be causing some of this. You might also be part of what going on. After all, we were *both* in the lower hallway when the lockers slammed."

"I still say that the whole thing is whack, so what are you saying we should do?"

"We need to meet away from this school."

"That shouldn't be too hard." I grinned smugly. "You live right down the street from me!"

"Ah," she said, "that *was* you walking the dog in the little park the other night. Good! Getting together after school should not be a problem. Here, give me your cell number. I will text you, and we can work out a time."

"Okay."

"I have got to go now. Your research was good, and you looked at every possible explanation. That was smart."

She tossed the stapled pages onto the worktable. "I think you should look at that one a little more closely."

I turned to look at the pages she tossed, and suddenly she was walking out of the room. There was a smile on her face. "I'll text you."

I leaned against the table, a little drained and confused. *What just happened?* I asked myself. I had more questions than answers.

I picked up the article Penelope had singled out. The title read "EM Fluctuations and Poltergeist Phenomena" by Dr. Mikhail Dredalus, professor emeritus, Columbia University School of Psychology; curator, Ironwood Museum of Antiquities.

As I said, more questions than answers.

Chapter 7

Microfish

"POLTER . . . WHAT?"
"Geists, poltergeists. *It's* German or something. It means *mischievous ghost* or something like that."

"*Ghosts*! Dude, I think that Penny Dreadful is whacked out!"

"Air!" I was starting to get exasperated. "First, don't call her Penny Dreadful, and second, she's not whacked out, and third, *you weren't there!*" My index finger underscored each word with a jab to his chest. "And don't call me *dude*!"

"Hey, that hurts!"

"Sorry, but I'm telling you it was weird. All those lockers opening and slamming shut and the air turning so cold . . . that's also a classic sign of some kind of *paranormal* activity."

"What if she was pranking you? That's possible too!"

"But why would she? What does it get her?"

"I don't know, attention or something," he said, still rubbing his chest.

I studied Air's face for a minute. Maybe he was right; maybe I was getting caught up in some weird game this Penny Dreadful was playing. It made sense—the whole *gothic* thing she had going on and the mysterious Eastern European accent. Heck, maybe *that* wasn't even real.

"No, I was there, and she didn't know I was following her until everything started to *go weird*."

"Hey, whatever. I'm jus' saying."

"I know, Alonzo [I used his real name when I was being *totally serious*], and I appreciated it, but really, something is going on. Something like we've never experienced before. I just know it!"

Air just stared at me.

I didn't hear from Penelope until Sunday. She texted me.

KC,

We nd 2g2 d pub lib n l%k N2 twn hx. cn u MMA my hous @ 2 p.m.? r drivR Gustav cn drV us der.

[We need to go to the public library and look into town history. Can you meet me at my house at 2:00 p.m.? Our driver, Gustave, can drive us there.]

P.

Hey, I wasn't going to pass up a chance to get a ride in a limo, so I texted her back that I'd have to check with my mom and get back to her.

Mom, of course, wasn't with the idea of me getting into a strange limo with a driver she'd never met, so she offered to drive us.

Moms always spoil the fun, but I agreed and texted Penelope back.

I guess her parents had the same problem, so she said she'd meet me at the library.

When Mom and I pulled up in front of the library, Penelope was already there, standing near the front entrance.

"Okay, Mom. There she is. Thanks."

"Hold on, KC. Should I meet her, say hello . . . She looks like an interesting girl."

Whenever someone didn't quite meet with my mom's approval, she would call them interesting.

"Maybe some other time . . . We have a lot of research to do on this history project." That was my cover story.

"Okay then," she said reluctantly. "I'll pick you up right here in three hours."

"5:00 p.m. check, 'bye!" I bolted before she had a chance to think of anything else to say.

It was a warm early September day; I had on a T-shirt, capri pants, and flip-flops. Penelope was wearing a sleeveless black blouse, a black skirt, black leggings, and black shoes, which looked a lot like ballet slippers. A gauzy black shawl was draped over her left shoulder. Her black leather backpack hung from her other shoulder.

I ran up to her with a big smile. "Hi."

She smiled back. "Hello. Ready to go in?" She glanced over my shoulder and waved.

I turned to see my mom still parked at the curb, waving back.

"Is that your mother?"

"Yup, that's her."

"She looks nice."

"She's a mom. Y'know how that is."

Penelope suddenly looked a little sad. "We should go in."

I turned to give my mother another wave, and she drove off. As we started up the steps, I turned to Penelope.

"Why *exactly* are we here?"

"Did you look over that article I pulled out from your other research?"

"Yes, was it written by a relative of yours?"

"My father."

"Are you telling me that you think that Richelieu school has *poltergeists?*"

"That's what I thought at first, but I have a feeling it is something else."

"Meaning . . ."

"KC, I think that Richelieu High School is haunted."

Just then, a woman with two small kids was exiting the library. Penelope pulled me off to the side of the entrance steps, well away from the doors.

"KC, I don't know what you think about ghosts, but it is my father's work, and I have been with him on many *paranormal investigations.*"

I think my jaw must have dropped because she put her hand on my shoulder as if she was reassuring me. "I never actually saw any kind of ghost. My point is, that equipment I had the other day is accurate. It is designed for this kind of thing. My father uses it in his work. And between the readings I was getting and what we saw with our own to eyes—"

"And felt with my shins," I inserted.

"There is every indication that our school is haunted."

I folded my arms and leaned on one hip. I must have looked as if I was giving her attitude. And I was. Air's warning kept repeating in my head. I wasn't buying all this *paranormal* stuff.

"Listen, KC, believe what you will, but I do know this. People are *more* than what their bodies are made of. Call it a soul, the mind, chi, *the Force,* or whatever you wish. There is something else inside of us. Have you ever been in a crowd or driving in a car and suddenly turned your head to find that someone was looking at you?"

"Yes."

"That is a small example of what I'm talking about. There was a connection that was outside your five senses. You knew someone was watching you because you felt that energy, that *soul*."

"Okay," I said, "but how does this figure into what happened at the school?"

"I think that each of us leaves something behind . . . maybe that spirit only stays for a short time before it moves on. But for some people, that *something* is stronger. It stays behind for a longer amount of time."

"But why?" I asked. None of this was making a lot of sense to me.

"I'm not sure," she admitted. "Perhaps there is no *one* reason. For some, maybe it is the force of their personality. For others, perhaps it is that their loved ones won't let them go, and for others, as many believe, it is the events that surround their death or because of tragedies that occurred while they were alive. In almost every investigation my father has gone on, the haunting always seemed to be related to some tragic event."

"I get it, so we're here to see what might have happened at Richelieu school."

"Exactly."

"Okay, I'm done with that. Let's do some ghost hunting."

"Okay!"

Penelope thought that the best place would have been in the archives of newspapers, which really made a lot of sense. But it was a big job. I knew that nothing tragic had happened since I went to the school. I was sure that if something really bad had occurred in the last five years or so, I might have heard about it. We skimmed through digital archives of newspapers that ran back over ten years. There were plenty of stories mentioning the school, but they were mostly sports-related items, special cultural events, that sort of stuff. When we got back to the eighties, we found that the digital records stopped.

We went to the main desk to find an elderly woman cataloging some returned books. She was wearing a gray sweater over a pearl-colored blouse and a moss green skirt. A little name tag on her sweater stated that her name was Agnes Perault.

We asked her how we could research old newspapers that weren't in the computer database. She told us that we'd have to use the microfiche library in the research loft for newspapers older than 1991. I was confused; I had no idea what a *microfiche* was. But I followed her and Penelope into the research section. This area of the library seemed as if it was an afterthought. It was ugly and filled with musty old journals and magazines and newspapers, all crammed into a three-level area connected by stairs. The microfiche section was on the top floor, tucked off in a little corner between some bookcases. The microfiche library had its own catalog, which Mrs. Perault showed us how to use. A microfiche is like a tiny photo negative that contains super small versions of original documents. Each microfiche was kept in a plastic sleeve, which was yellowing with age. The sleeves were labeled by year and publication and catalog number. The microfiches were kept in big metal cabinets with drawers that creaked horribly when you pulled them out. We had to use these noisy, old-fashioned microfiche readers to see the negatives blown up full size. Each film contained four pages of photographed newspaper. What I wouldn't have given to be able to do a word search.

We searched through the microfiche library for nearly two hours, and we found nothing, not even a hint of any tragedy at our school. My nose was itching like crazy from the dust, my neck hurt, and I was ready to give up.

When I told Penelope that I was just about ready to call it a day, she blinked as if trying to understand what I was saying.

"But, KC, we've just barely gone through the late '80s. This might take some time. We have got to stay at it!"

I looked at her, amazed. "But why? I mean, why is it so urgent?"

She leaned closer. "It's nothing I can prove, KC, but I have this feeling that it's going to get worse. I had this feeling of anger down in that hallway."

"It sure sounded angry, duh!" I replied.

"Exactly!" she exclaimed, ignoring my wisecrack. "This is why we must find out what, if anything, created this *haunting*."

I sat back in my chair, exhausted. I liked Penelope, and I thought she was being honest with me despite a little voice in my head (which sounded a lot like Air's voice) telling me that this whole ghost-hunting thing was whack and bogus.

"Well," she said, "we can always come back if you don't think you can continue today."

I was glad that she was being sensible, but before I could reply, Mrs. Perault, the librarian, came up to us. "Girls," she said, "the library closes at five on Sundays, and it's nearly that now. You'll have to bring the microfiche sleeves back to the circulation desk so they can be refiled." She scanned the pile of sleeves that had accumulated between us. "My, you girls have been busy. What are you researching?"

I'm the kind of girl who never lets an opportunity to do less work slip by, so I thought maybe the librarian could help narrow the search.

"We're doing a history paper on our school, and we're trying to find out about any unusual, even tragic events that might have occurred at our school."

"What school do you go to?"

"Richelieu High School . . ."

"Oh my," said the librarian. The blood seemed to drain from her face. She was silent for a moment, and then she seemed to recover herself. "Well, there was a kitchen fire back in the '30s, but no one was hurt. But they did have to close the school."

"But that wasn't what you were thinking of, was it, Mrs. Perault?" said Penelope.

"Excuse me . . . What do you mean, young lady?"

"Just that I don't feel that a kitchen fire over seventy years ago would make you *blanch!*"

All I could think about was, *Who uses the word* blanch?

Mrs. Perault's hand shot up to her face. "Young lady, you're being rude!"

"I don't mean to be, ma'am, but we really have to know what you were reminded of."

"That is none of your concern, young lady. Come on now, gather up the films!"

"Mrs. Perault, please!" said Penelope.

Mrs. Perault looked at Penelope for what seemed like five minutes. With a determined look on her face, she walked over to the microfiche catalog and looked up an entry. Without hesitation, she retrieved a single microfiche.

"It is against my better judgment to share this with you, but I have the feeling that you are an earnest young lady and that you have a good reason for asking me about something I've been trying to forget for fifty-one years!"

Penelope and I just looked at each other while Mrs. Perault loaded the microfiche into the reader. She moved the flat film under the viewfinder.

"Here it is," she said. "There wasn't much of a mention of it in the paper. The school and the police and the families that were involved wanted to keep everything as quiet as possible."

Penelope and I crowded over the viewer, trying to read the article. The headline read, STUDENT'S DEATH RESULT OF FAULTY EQUIPMENT.

An inquest determined that Sarah Jane McCormack died as a result of a faulty mechanism controlling the movable flooring covering a newly installed swimming pool in the lower level of the Colonel Francois Richelieu School on Addams Avenue in White Plains. While it is still undetermined how the high school senior gained access to the pool area after school hours, the coroner can only speculate that she somehow gained access to the pool area and activated the mechanism that controlled the floor. Ms. McCormack fell into the pool, struck her head, and drowned. Several other students, many from prominent local families, are being questioned, but their names have been withheld due to their age. The school has determined that the pool represents a safety issue, and it will permanently close the pool. While the school board maintains that adequate safeguards were installed, the McCormack family has started proceedings against the school and the designers and installers of the pool.

The article went on, but we were too numb to read more. We turned toward Mrs. Perault. There were tears in her eyes, her voice cracked. "Sarah Jane McCormack was my best friend. She was an A student and would never have gone into that pool area without permission. I don't know what happened, but I do know that it was more that an accident. Now you have to tell me, what are you girls looking for and why?"

Penelope walked up to Mrs. Perault and took the older woman's hand. "I don't think Sarah Jane is at peace."

Chapter 8

Security Cameras

A S PENELOPE AND I left the library, we were in a state of shock. Well, at least I was. Penelope seemed calmer and more mysterious than ever.

I grabbed her by the arm at the top of the steps and turned her toward me.

"Oh my gosh, that was too freaky," I said.

"It was unusual, unexpected, yes, but not completely freaky. I was hoping to meet someone who might have attended the Richelieu School over the last fifty years. It seems that luck was on our side."

"And you don't call *that* freaky?"

"Yes, I suppose it was."

I was getting a little impatient with her. "And what do you *suppose* is going on at the school?" I demanded.

She looked past me at some point too distant to see.

"I don't know," she said as she absentmindedly walked around me. "I don't know, but I will."

I turned to watch her walk away. There at the curb was the black Mercedes-Benz I'd seen at her house. Penelope got in quickly, and the limo drove away. I stood there staring after her like a geek.

The next few weeks were filled with school and homework and meeting new kids. Everyone had settled into the new school year. I barely saw Penelope Dredalus during those weeks. She sat quietly in class, and when the bell rang, she would gather her books and immediately disappear into the crowded hallway. We spoke occasionally, but it was always awkward. I could tell that she didn't want to talk about what we had learned at the library. In some weird way, I was mad at her. I felt as if she was dissing me with the silent treatment. She had gotten me involved in this *weirdness* and then dropped me.

I wasn't getting along too well with Air either. He had met some other skateboarders and was spending more and more time with them. We still

. . . We were all shocked to see what looked like every chair in the school neatly arranged on the lawn of the school.

talked, but things were different. I guess that's the way things go. You start to make new friends, and suddenly your old friends and even your "not so old" friends start to be less important except I didn't feel as if I was the one who was changing. I felt as if everyone else was changing. Things were getting so confusing!

The leaves started to change too, and suddenly the days felt as if they were getting shorter, and there was a chill in the air. It was October, my favorite month. I loved the fall, and I loved Halloween. At least one of my friends would have a party, and there was also a Halloween dance at our school. This year, Halloween was on a Friday, so the dance would probably be on the same night. Going to a school dance was way better than sitting on the front porch handing out candy, which was usually how I spent my Halloween since I became too old to trick or treat.

Ghostwise, things weren't exactly quiet. One morning as the school buses were pulling into Richelieu High School, we were all shocked to see what looked like every chair in the school neatly arranged on the lawn of the school. Everyone on the bus laughed, thinking that it was some crazy Halloween prank. I wasn't so sure. But it did get us the day off as the school staff returned the chairs and made sure that nothing else was out of place. They even called the police to investigate for vandalism.

There were a few more loud bangs in the lower hallways, but people were starting to get used to it. The teachers said that the noises had something to do with the heating system. There were always guys in the school with coveralls checking out the ducts and the hall thermostats. The heating system was beyond the skills of the head janitor, Mr. Foote. So they had a bunch of technicians come into the school to help Mr. Foote track down the problem.

The school was also having a new security system installed. One of the installers was really creepy. He had this huge bushy mustache and greasy black hair and was always skulking around the stairwell that led to the basement.

After the incident in the basement and what we learned from Mrs. Perault at the library, I was on edge. Sometimes, I'd feel as if I was being watched, and I'd turn around and see either Penelope with one of her gadgets or the creepy installer guy. It occurred to me that they were watching *me*, but I couldn't understand why they would, so I tried to put it out of my mind.

And there were other odd things. A few times as I was going to math or Spanish class on the first floor and I'd pass the stairwell leading to the basement, I'd catch a glimpse of Mr. Foote just standing at the bottom of the stairs as if he were listening for something. Just standing there listening, totally unaware of his surroundings, weird!

About a week after the chair incident, I was launching myself up the central stairs going to science class when there was a huge crash. It shook the entire school, and it seemed to come from everywhere. Before I knew it, there was Penelope running down the same stairs toward me.

"KC, I'm glad you're here. I need your help!"

"B-but I've got science class."

"After that crash, they'll probably evacuate the whole school! We haven't much time!"

"Time for *what*?"

"Just before the sound, there was a huge spike in the air pressure, just like the last time. And you can see on my EM detectors that there is a strong concentration of waves coming from below us."

I nodded yes, but I couldn't read the thingy she was holding in front of my face.

Students and teachers were already starting to fill the hallways; some of them looked scared.

"Come on. We've got to get downstairs!" she said as she pulled me by the sleeve.

"What! No way! I'm not going down there again."

"You have to. I need you as a witness."

"I *don't* have to, and besides, a witness to what?"

"KC, PLEASE! There's no time, and I need you to come with me."

I guess I'm an idiot because I shouldered my backpack and started running after her.

With all the confusion, no one stopped us, and we made it to the basement stairwell in a few minutes. Penelope kept the EM device in front of her. In my jostling view, I could see the glowing waves moving across the screen faster and faster, and the dark blue color on the screen was turning to a lighter and lighter blue.

We flew down the stairs and stopped at the section where the lockers had slammed themselves shut a few weeks earlier.

"This is it!" Penelope said, looking at her instrument. "This is the psychic center of the disturbance."

"Can you feel the air pressure?" I was almost yelling.

"Yes, and it's rising fast."

My ears started to feel as if I was swimming ten feet underwater. I covered them with my hands.

"I feel it too!" she said.

I grabbed her arm. "We better get out of here!" I was looking at Penelope, and over her shoulder I saw a movement in the shadows of the long, dark basement hallway. She must have seen the look of surprise on my face because she wheeled around to see what I was looking at. It was unmistakable. It was Mr. Foote staggering down the hall away from us. For a brief second, he turned back to look at us; an expression of pale horror played over his face.

Just then, there was a scream from upstairs. We looked at each other and bolted back up the stairs. When we got to the top, the hall was filled with students, crowding around someone lying on the floor. We pushed our way through just as Mr. Foote, the custodian, and the principal, Mr. Cortez, were entering the circle from the other side.

"Everyone back. Give her air."

I looked down to see Denise Soong, a junior varsity cheerleader, crumpled on the floor, crying.

"Over there," she screamed, pointing to the direction we just came from. "I saw it over there!" Tears were streaming down her face, and her hands were trembling. It was clear that she was really scared.

Everyone turned to follow her pointing finger. The only thing any of us could see was the hallway and the top of the lower-level stairs.

"What, Denise?" said Mr. Cortez, helping her up. "There's nothing there."

She looked up at the principal and over toward the stairs. "There was *something* there, a dark shadow coming up the stairs. It came right toward me. It was so cold I screamed!"

Mr. Cortez scanned the gathered students. "Did anyone else see anything?" One little nerdy eighth grader pointed at Penelope and me.

"I saw them coming up the stairs just a second after she screamed."

Mr. Cortez walked over to us. He was a tall, intimidating man.

"Did either one of you young ladies see anything?"

We both answered no. Mr. Cortez looked at us, rubbing his chin.

"Aren't you the two who were on the lower level when the lockers slammed shut last month?"

We both nodded yes.

"You're both coming to the office with me." Then he turned around addressing the students gathered around us.

"I don't know what's going on here, but it seems to me that it's a little early for trick or treat. If any of you are involved in some elaborate prank, I guarantee I will find out, and there will be trouble. You two, follow me!"

Mr. Cortez walked us through the crowd. I glanced back, and behind the students, I got a glimpse of the creepy installer guy standing at the top of the stairs, watching.

Mr. Cortez ushered us into his sunny office then left immediately without saying a word. It seemed as if we were sitting in Mr. Cortez's office for hours. Neither Penelope nor I said a word to each other. In fact, we barely looked at each other. I was miffed at her for getting me into the whole situation. I think she could sense it. She just sat there silently, staring at the floor. Several times, she carefully revealed the display of her EM detector to check and see if anything was happening. I'd glance over at her through the corner of my eye. I didn't want to give her the satisfaction that I was interested in her and her whacked tech toys.

When Mr. Cortez finally returned, I was pretty much ready to plead guilty to whatever he thought I was guilty of just to get out of there.

"Well, ladies, I think you have some explaining to do."

We both sat there silently, looking at him.

"Doesn't it seem odd that we had another *unexplained phenomenon* and you two were close by?"

"I-I suppose it does," I said. "But honestly, we had nothing to do with the loud crash or whatever scared Denise."

"But you were both close by and downstairs when those lockers slammed, where, I should also add, you weren't supposed to be. I've been a principal for a long time, Ms. Watson. This just doesn't *smell* right."

"Mr. Cortez," said Penelope, "to be perfectly honest, we weren't supposed to be downstairs, but when we heard the loud crash, we ran straight for the lower level. We were trying to investigate what might have caused the crash."

Mr. Cortez turned a little red and glared at Penelope. "My point exactly. You were downstairs without permission. It's all very suspicious. If this is some kind of early Halloween prank . . ." His voice trailed off, letting the implied threat sink in.

"But we didn't do anything!" I blurted out. "We were leaving class when the crash happened. We had nothing to do with that!"

There was a knock on the door. The door opened out into the main office outside Mr. Cortez's private office. As the door swung back, I caught a glimpse of a rather large bulbous nose and a bushy black mustache; it was the creepy installer guy.

"Mr. Cortez, luckily, the security cameras are now online. I have the entire *incident* recorded." His accent was thick, like someone pretending to be *Count Dracula*. These two were nowhere near the stairs when the first crash occurred and nowhere near where the girl fainted."

"Thank you, Mr. DuLac. I'll discuss this with you later."

Mr. DuLac managed to peek around the door at us then left, closing the door.

Mr. Cortez continued staring at the door for a heartbeat.

"Odd man," he muttered to himself. "Well, I guess you ladies are exonerated by the newly installed surveillance system. But I'm going to be watching you both, *and* no more wandering around the school without permission. Please see Mrs. Costanzia for a hall pass." He turned toward his computer monitor, dismissing us.

When we had finally left the office, permission slips in hand, it was nearing the end of last period. I started down the hall toward my locker without saying anything to Penelope.

"KC," she said, coming up behind me, "I know that you are angry with me. I'm sorry I brought you along." I turned back toward her, controlling my anger.

"Listen, Penelope, if my mom catches wind of this, I'm in trouble. I really don't want to have anything to do with your *paranormal whatever* anymore, 'kay? Later."

I threw my hands up and stomped off down the hall. I glanced back once to see Penelope still standing there, looking at me, then she turned to walk the other way. Beyond her was creepy Mr. DuLac standing on a tall ladder, tending to one of the security cameras.

Chapter 9

Bad Video

AFTER SPENDING MOST of the afternoon in the principal's office, I looked forward to the long, dull school bus ride home. I made my way to the rear and threw myself into an empty seat. The driver was starting to close the folding door just as Air bounded on. I sank down even lower into my seat, hoping he wouldn't see me. He spotted me, smiled, and started down the aisle toward me.

He fell heavily into the seat beside me and said, "Hey."

"Hey," I said back and stared out the window.

Air wasn't giving up; he had something on his mind. "So what's up?"

I swung around and faced him. "You probably heard . . ."

"I heard you guys had to go to Cortez's office."

"That's right. Y'know why?"

"Grapevine says you guys scared Denise Soong. She like fainted or something."

"I'm not sure about that, but she was scared . . . But it was nothing that we did!" It sounded funny to me to refer to Penelope and me as "we."

Air picked up on it too. "*We*? Yeah, you and Penny Dreadful, you guys are pretty tight, huh? BFFs, right?"

"Not likely!" I said probably a little too strongly. "OMG, ever since I started hangin' with her, some weird stuff has happened. My mom is going to kill me when she finds out that I went to the principal's office."

"I guess," said Air.

"I guess," I said and turned back to look out the window.

"Look, KC, I know things have been a little weird between us lately, but I've just got this feeling that whatever Penny's into, it could mean danger and trouble. Please be careful."

I looked at Air as if I'd never really seen him before. Suddenly the skateboarder was gone, and this guy was in his place. Suddenly he was sweet and caring and somehow more *grown-up*.

"Thanks, Alonzo. I'll be careful. After today, I'll probably be grounded until spring recess. That'll definitely keep me out of trouble!" I giggled at the serious look on Air's face, and I gave him a gentle shove.

Neither of us said anything else until we came to our stop. We both got off, said good-bye, and went our separate ways.

As I passed Penelope's house, I promised myself I wouldn't look at her house. I was still upset with her. I blamed her for getting us in trouble, but I knew that the truth was that the loud noises and Denise getting scared had nothing to do with anything Penelope had done. I stopped and sighed and hitched up my backpack. I glanced over at her house just as a couple of the upstairs curtains moved. Was that her? Was she home already, waiting for me to get home? I put it out of my mind and kept walking.

When I got home, Mom and my little brother were getting ready to leave. "Hey, where are you guys going?"

"Dentist," said James, looking really glum.

"Do you want to come with us, sweetie?" said my mom. "You can keep me company."

"I kind of wanted to chill and get a jump on my homework."

Mom looked at me with a quizzical look on her face. "Anything wrong, KC?" she asked.

"Not really," I said, trying to look innocent.

"Well, okay. We'll see you in about an hour."

She placed her hand on the top of James's head and ushered him out the door.

I sighed. I knew that that uncanny sixth sense of hers had picked up some vibe from me. I also knew that the school hadn't called her. So suddenly not only did I get sent down to the principal's office, but I now had a moral dilemma on my hands—to tell or not to tell.

Twenty minutes later, I was sitting at the island in the kitchen, enjoying a bowl of ice cream and pondering all this when there was a noise at the front door. I could hear steps on the front porch, a pause, then the doorbell rang. Even though I was aware that someone was there, I still jumped when the doorbell rang.

"Who is it?" I asked.

"Penelope."

"Great," I muttered to myself.

I took a deep breath and opened the door.

"Hi," I said.

"Hello, KC . . . Do you have a couple of minutes to talk?"

I was not in the mood for this, but I was raised to be polite. "Come on in." I motioned for her to enter. Penelope stepped past me and looked back at me for some instruction as to where to go next.

"Just go straight back to the kitchen." I pointed vaguely. "I was having some ice cream. Want some?"

"Yes, please, if you don't mind."

I did. I was still mad at her, but that polite thing was still in effect. "Have a seat at the counter. I'll get you a bowl."

"Listen, KC, I just wanted to say that I'm sorry I got you in trouble today, but I really needed you with me."

"Why?"

I didn't think she was expecting me to ask that. She sat their quietly, just looking at me. I handed her a bowl of tricolored ice cream. She scooped up some vanilla and spooned it into her mouth.

"I needed you there because I trust you."

"Why . . . ?"

"I just trust you to be there, to make the right choices, to be strong even if you're afraid."

"Well, Penelope, you really don't know me that well . . . Aren't you expecting a lot from me?"

She looked at me and spooned in another helping of vanilla. She held the spoon daintily up in the air as the ice cream melted in her mouth. "I guess I am . . . But I also know that you're someone I can rely on . . . And besides, I like you." She spooned in another mouthful and sat there looking at me, relishing the cool vanilla.

Suddenly I was a little uncomfortable. She was opening up to me a little, but I was still a little mad at her for getting me in trouble.

"I see you like vanilla," I said, changing the subject. "I would have expected you to like something—"

"A little darker? Like licorice-flavored ice cream perhaps?" she said with a faint smirk on her face.

"Well," I said, looking down, a little embarrassed, "yeah, something like that."

"I know my dress is a little odd, but I don't believe that it's any more peculiar than some of the *goths* at school."

"Probably a whole lot more normal, just a little—"

"Somber?" she finished my sentence.

"Yes, *somber* would be one word for it. Another might be *gloomy*."

"You are very observant, KC. *Gloomy* would be a good description of my dress." Suddenly a sad, faraway look came across her face. She looked directly at me in an effort to ignore whatever it was that was making her sad. "KC, I'm here because I have something very important to show you. It concerns these strange things happening at our school. It concerns the very unhappy spirit of Sarah Jane McCormack."

My jaw must have dropped. I couldn't believe that she was still thinking about that stuff.

"You looked shocked, KC. Why?"

"I thought you were here to apologize, not start up with this spook stuff!"

"I wouldn't use the term *spook stuff*, but that's exactly what's going on, and I think that we've only seen the beginning of what might be happening."

I have to admit that I felt like dumping the ice cream bowl right on top of her head, but she had my attention. "Okay, I give up! What *are* you talking about?"

"I'd rather show you. Could you come to my house?"

"When . . . ? Why?"

"Tonight," she said, "to look at a very disturbing video."

Chapter 10

333 Whitney Street

OKAY, I ADMIT it. I was way too curious to see Penelope's house, but I really had my doubts. It was a school night, so it took a bit of convincing to get Mom to let me go. Some small part of me wished that she would say no, but of course, she said it would be fine as long as I was home by nine thirty. It was seven thirty, and the sky was dark as I walked down Battle Avenue and turned onto Whitney Street. I walked up to the front door of 333 and rang the doorbell.

I heard Penelope call out to someone that she would answer the door. I assumed that she was talking to the butler, Gustave. How cool was that? She actually had a butler. She opened the heavy door and flashed me a big smile.

"Come in, please. I am happy that you came." She was still dressed in the same clothes she wore at school. "Let's go to the study. There we can look at the video."

She led me through the foyer, through another set of doors, and into the main hall of her house. I must have gasped because she turned around to look at me with an odd look on her face.

"Is anything the matter, KC?"

"No, ah yeah . . . This room is so . . . big. It looks so much bigger than it does on the outside."

In front of us was a wide central staircase leading to a balcony that ran around three sides of the hall. There were doors along the balcony leading to other rooms, and in the center of the rear wall was another smaller staircase. There were lots of tapestries and old Greek statues and paintings with heavily carved frames.

Penelope giggled. "Everyone says the same thing. It's an illusion, I think."

"I guess . . ."

"Come. The study is over this way."

We walked through another set of heavy doors that opened from the center and slid into the wall.

"Wow," I said, "sick doors."

"Yes . . . sick." She obviously wasn't too comfortable with slanguage. "This is the study. I guess it's pretty sick too."

"No, I'd say it's *tight*."

The study was another big room, lined with bookshelves that were filled with dusty old books. There were several big mahogany tables in the room; one was piled high with books and some kind of clay tablet. Near the tablet was a magnifying glass and a notepad filled with funny little letters. Another had several workstations, laptops, and towers and some other equipment I was not familiar with. There was a large bay window at the far end of the room, framed in dark velvety curtains. Directly in front of the windows was a carved desk with a small lamp on it. I jumped a little when I realized that someone was sitting at the desk, a man, his tweed jacket barely visible in the little pool of light given off by a small lamp shaded in green glass.

"Oh, Papa," said Penelope. "This is my friend KC."

The man stood up, still in the heavy shadow. "Good evening, KC," he said in a heavier version of Penelope's accent. "Welcome to our home."

"Thank you, sir."

"Papa, may KC and I use the study for a short while?"

"Ah yes, of course, you have much homework. I am done for the evening. I only ask that you do not go near the tablet."

"Yes, Papa, of course."

Dr. Dredalus stepped out from behind the desk, still hidden by shadow. He was tall and thin. As he walked quickly past us and exited through the pocket doors, I caught a glimpse of the same olive complexion as his daughter and long but neatly trimmed black hair streaked with silver.

Penelope stepped over to the pocket doors and closed them behind her father then turned toward the table with the electronic equipment. She sat down in front of the large LCD screen. She reached over and pulled another chair.

"Please sit," she said.

I did and looked at her, waiting.

"KC, you might not believe what I'm going to show you. But it is real."

"Look, Penelope, can we cut to the chase? Just show the video."

"Okay . . . as you will. Here it goes."

She clicked at the dock at the bottom of the screen, and a window popped up to the center of the monitor. The image was a black-and-white

BOB BERRY

. . . I realized that someone was sitting at the desk, a man, his tweed jacket barely visible in the little pool of light given off by a small lamp shaded in green glass.

image of . . . one of the hallways at our school. "Hey!" I said. "How did you get this?"

"That isn't important. Just watch."

She clicked on the Play button in the window, and I saw the progress bar at the bottom of the frame start to move. The hall didn't change for several minutes except for the blurry figure of Mr. Foote, the custodian, moving through the frame. Then there was another long pause before anything happened. At first, I was straining my eyes, looking hard to see something, and then a faint figure seemed to resolve out of the video noise of the frame. It was undefined at first, but slowly the image sharpened into the unmistakable figure of a girl in some kind of big-skirted dress. The figure faded back into the blurred hallway. I could feel the hair on my neck and shoulders standing on end. I turned toward Penelope.

"Watch," she said.

As I looked back, Mr. Foote reentered the scene, pushing a large broom on the granite floor. As he passed, the figure seemed to ooze out of the background and loom over the clueless janitor. Now the face on the figure was clearly distorted in a face of rage.

"Where did you get this?" I stammered.

"I can't tell you that, but I can tell you that this is not the only one with that . . . *apparition*." The word sent chills down my spine. "But I can tell you that I've seen four other images similar to this. In every case, Mr. Foote is in the shot. This was shot only minutes before Mr. Foote went running past us in the basement and the last 'event' occurred."

I must have been dim. I felt as if I should have been getting this, but I wasn't. "So what does it all mean? Mr. Foote was in the hallway when we got up the stairs . . . He was white as a sheet. Why didn't he tell Principal Cortez that he'd seen something too?"

Penelope looked at me. "I don't know the answer to that, but I'm fairly convinced that it is Mr. Foote that is being haunted."

I sat back. It took me a minute to get her words straight in my head. "But why Mr. Foote?"

"That, my dear Watson, is what we need to discover."

"Huh?"

"That is what we need to figure out."

Chapter 11

The Question of Mr. Foote

I WAS TOTALLY clueless about finding out what the connection was between Mr. Foote and the "apparition," as Penelope called it. Luckily, she seemed to have a mind made for storing this kind of stuff, and she remembered something from the articles we read at the library over a month ago.

"That last article Mrs. Perault showed us said that 'several other students, many from prominent local families, are being questioned,' but none of their names were given in the article because they were all minors. I think we need to talk to Mrs. Perault again."

"I don't think she really enjoyed talking last time. What makes you think she'll talk to you now? This whole thing is a sensitive issue for her."

Penelope leaned back in her chair and put her hand on her chin.

"You are correct, KC, but we'll have to try. There may be lives at stake here."

We sat there quietly for a few minutes, the computers humming away and the big grandfather clock in the corner clicking away the minutes.

Gustave appeared in the doorway startling us—well, at least me.

"Miss, it's getting late, and I know that you still have several study assignments to complete," he said in a thick German accent.

"Would Ms. Watson want me to drive her home?"

I looked at Penelope.

"It's very close, Gustave. Perhaps we can walk her home."

"Very good, miss."

And so they did. Gustave stayed a little behind us as we walked and talked over some lame school stuff. When we got to my front porch, I said good night and watched Penelope and her butler walk back up to 333 Whitney Street.

When I got in, Mom and James were finishing his homework, and Dad was down in his basement shop tinkering with something.

"KC, Air called. I told him you'd call him back. How did it go? How was the house?"

"Big, and kinda creepy."

"Did you meet Mr. Dredalus?"

"*Doctor*, Mom . . . Dr. Dredalus."

"*Excuse* me. Well, did you meet *Dr.* Dredalus?"

"Yup, I met him."

"*And . . .*"

"There is no *and*. He said hello and left."

I think part of me was being difficult on purpose; all the questions were getting annoying.

"Okay . . . Well, you'd better call Air back before it gets too late."

I guess she got the hint that I wasn't in the mood to give her the whole skinny on my visit to Penelope's house. But what the heck was with Air? He seemed to call me every time I was with Penelope. I went upstairs and called him from my room.

"Air?"

"KC? What's up?"

"I don't know. I'm returning your call."

"Oh yeah. So what's up?"

"*Air . . .*"

"Oh, sorry. I was just, y'know, touching base."

"Touching base? Since when do you 'touch base'?"

"I don't know, It's just that we don't hang like we used to, so I thought I'd give you a call."

Air seemed nervous, but I was starting to get into one of my difficult moods. "Okay, well, everything's good here." I was hoping that that was all he wanted to hear and then he'd say good night.

"KC?"

"Yes?"

"Mmm, there's something else . . ."

"Yes?"

"You going to the Halloween dance next Friday?"

Truth was, I hadn't much thought about it. "I don't know. Are you?"

"I was thinking maybe I would."

"Cool."

"I was thinking maybe you could go with me?"

"Huh?"

"You know . . . like on a date?"

"Say what?"

"KC, give me a break! I'm asking you if you want to go to the Halloween dance with me at the school next Friday night."

I didn't know how to answer. I just sat there, silent.

"KC, I know you're there. I can still hear you breathing."

"Yeah, I'm here."

"Well, what do you say . . . Come on. This is hard enough."

I heard the pleading in his voice, and it snapped me out of my shock. But how was I going to handle this? Suddenly everything between us was different; I mean, Air wanted to go on a date *with me*! And I wasn't sure how I felt about him, especially as a date.

"Wow, Air, I wasn't expecting this . . . You're asking me out on a date?"

"Duh?"

"Can I just think about it?"

"Huh . . . Come on, KC . . . It's just me, and it's just going to a dance. Heck, we went to them in fifth grade. It was no big deal?"

But that's where Air was wrong. It was a big deal, at least it was to me. This was my first high school dance, and I never even considered being asked to a dance by Air. Not that I was really expecting anyone else to ask, but definitely not Air. And it wasn't because I didn't like him. I did. It was just that he was my friend, not my boyfriend.

He obviously was getting a little annoyed with my silence. I heard him sigh a couple of times.

"Look, KC, think it over and let me know, okay? Sorry to freak you out."

"No, it's not that . . ."

"Look, don't worry about it. I'll see you at school tomorrow. Good night." *Click.*

I fell back onto my bed and looked up at the ceiling. Were these the changes Mom kept going on about? I certainly understood all the physical stuff about growing up, but this emotional stuff was a whole other thing. And like any other teenager, I had crushes on a whole bunch of cute boys, but Air was never one of them. I wasn't sure if I liked him that way. I mean, he was my friend, and I was more comfortable with him than any boy I knew. And he was kind of cute in a scruffy skateboarder way, but did I *like* like him? It was all so complicated. And the worst of it was that I completely blew it and hurt Air's feelings. Part of me wanted to go down and talk it over with Mom, but then I thought that maybe I was better off trying to figure this out on my own.

The next day at school, Air kind of avoided me. But as he got off the bus, he glanced over at me and gave me a quick smile.

When I got home, I checked my e-mail. Amphoragirl was at the top of my inbox.

KC,

> *I've bn n tuch W ms. Perault, she'll C us, bt nt @ d lib, RU available fri aftRnun?*
> [I've been in touch with Mrs. Perault. She'll see us but not at the library. Are you available Friday afternoon?]

P

See Mrs. Perault? The library lady?! What was she talking about? The last thing I wanted to do on a Friday afternoon was to sit in some old person's musty house discussing ghosts. Just then, my phone rang.

"KC?" It was Penelope. "Did you get my e-mail?"

"Just read it."

"Are you available?"

"Ah man . . . I don't know."

"KC, I need you there."

"But why? Why me?"

"As I said, I trust you, and you've been on this *investigation* from the start."

"*Investigation?*"

"That is how I think of it. Listen, KC, if I'm correct about what is happening, we could be dealing with a dangerous situation."

"But I still don't get it. Ghosts are wispy things that walk through walls, and they're real scary for sure, But how are they dangerous?"

"KC, this 'ghost' has proven to have powerful poltergeist-like abilities. This ghost is moving objects around on a grand scale, and its power is building. All my readings confirm this! Remember those devices I used to gauge air pressure, temperature, and electromagnetic levels?"

"Yeah."

"Well, I planted several of those devices in the school, and I'm getting readings that are growing in strength and area. They are no longer only appearing in the basement but now throughout the school."

BOB BERRY

"So I guess that you think that she was the one that took all the chairs out of the school?"

"I do. And I think that if this *is* the spirit of Sarah Jane McCormack, her power will reach full strength on Halloween, the night she died."

My mind was wandering to Air and our "to be determined" date.

"But we're still missing a piece in the puzzle," she continued.

"Which is?"

"Why are we seeing the strongest manifestations when Mr. Foote is nearby?"

"Well, like you said, Mr. Foote is being haunted."

"Yes, but *why?*"

"Which is why we have to talk to the library lady, right?"

"Mrs. Perault," she corrected me.

"Whatever . . ."

"So will you come with me?"

I breathed a heavy sigh into the phone. "Okay . . . I'll be your posse."

Chapter 12

The Library Lady

A FTER SOME PLEADING, I talked Mom into letting me go to
the mall with Penelope (under Gustave's supervision, of course),
and it wasn't a complete fib. We would go there *after* we interviewed the
library lady. I don't know how Penelope managed to get the meeting with
Mrs. Perault, but I was learning that she could be very persuasive.

Mrs. Perault's apartment was on the north side of White Plains in a co-op
complex off North Broadway. The inside was pretty much how I imagined
it would be. Small, cramped, and filled with dusty old knickknacks and the
smell of my grandma's perfume.

Mrs. Perault settled into an armchair and looked us over. "Honestly,
I don't understand the morbid fascination with Sarah Jane's death. Is this
some Halloween trick?"

"If only," I said.

"Mrs. Perault," said Penelope, "this is no prank. I have evidence that
there is a paranormal disturbance occurring at our school, and I believe
that it might concern your deceased friend."

"Nonsense."

"Mrs. Perault, perhaps you know the book of my father, Dr. Mikhail
Dredalus. He has written several scholarly books on the subject of the
paranormal, and he is, by no means, a trickster."

"Yes, he did a book signing years ago at our library."

"That was his first book. It was published a few months before I was born."

"My, that long ago?"

"Yes, when he and my mother still worked for the Columbia University
School of Psychology. They both lived on Battle Hill where my Father and
I live now.

"And your mother?"

"She's not with us."

I could see that Penelope's face looked pained at that small mention of
her mother.

The library lady seemed to pick up on it too. "All right, young lady. I'll try to answer your questions."

Penelope took out a legal pad from her backpack and prepared to write. "Mrs. Perault, the newspaper article you showed us mentioned that several other students were being questioned in Sarah Jane's death. But none were mentioned by name. Can you give me a list of those students who were questioned?"

"That's all you wanted to know? That's easy. I was questioned, Billy McDuff, George Cranston, Elizabeth Drake, and Elliot Foote."

Penelope and I instantly looked at each other.

"Mrs. Perault, do you know if any of these people work for the school system?"

"Let me think," she said, gently drumming her fingers on her chin. "I lost contact with Billy and George after graduation. Elizabeth worked for the school until she retired last year. I think Elliot worked for the school system as a bus driver or a custodian."

"Bingo!" I said.

"Excuse me?" said Mrs. Perault.

"There is a Mr. Foote at our school," said Penelope. "He serves as a custodian."

"That must be him," replied Mrs. Perault. "Although I would have thought that he'd be retired by now."

"Can you tell us anything else surrounding Sarah Jane's accident?" asked Penelope.

"No, I can't. I was at the school that night, but I stayed at the dance in the gymnasium. Sarah and the others I mentioned wandered off. I always thought that was odd because Sarah Jane wasn't really friends with any of them. They were with the 'popular crowd.' Sarah Jane and I and even Elliot were more serious students. We were all in the debate club, on the school newspaper, that sort of thing. That's why it was just so odd seeing Sarah Jane with those others leaving the gym together. They were laughing and having a grand time. She honestly looked as if she was having fun. She was excited as they were leaving. A half hour later, Elizabeth was running into the gym, hysterical. She was crying that there had been a terrible accident. It has become a vague memory over the years. I'm sorry."

Penelope smiled at the Mrs. Perault and shook her hand. "Thank you for trusting us and sharing your memories. You've helped a lot."

"You two, be careful. I'm not sure I believe in what you're suggesting, but Sarah Jane was very smart, and she always had such a bad temper."

When we left Mrs. Perrault's building, we were practically running.

"Hey, Penelope, what's the rush?"

"I have to get back to my father's study. There is something I must research."

"Whoa, girl!" I said, grabbing her by the forearm. "The deal was we see Library Lady then Gustave takes us to the mall."

"But there is so little time."

"Listen, it's Friday night. School's closed for the weekend. Nobody will be there, so no danger! Ol' Sarah Jane will just have to practice her mad haunting skills on herself."

Penelope chuckled. "I suppose that you are right."

"Yo, this is KC! You better believe I'm right. Besides, you'd make me into a liar if we didn't go. That was the cover story I gave my mom in order to see Mrs. Perault."

"You are right. I wouldn't want your mother to put you on the ground."

"Huh?" I stopped as I was getting into the Dredalus Mercedes.

"Put you on the ground, punish you."

"Oh, you mean grounded . . . Nah, we wouldn't want that, so the mall it is?"

Penelope threw herself into the backseat of the limo and buckled herself up. "Yes, to the mall it is! Gustave, to the mall, please!" And she gestured like a princess ordering a carriage. We both started giggling. Gustave looked even more deadpan, which made us laugh more.

"This is what I like best about Americans . . . You seem so carefree."

"We're not without worries . . . But we try to have fun. And we do love to shop even when we can't afford it!" We started laughing again.

"You know, KC, there is one other reason I want you on this *investigation*."

"Oh?"

"Yes, you are one of the few people who can make me laugh."

We arrived at the mall and headed straight to the clothes stores. I had a purse full of babysitting money that was dying to get out and be spent. Penelope saw some clothes she liked: a black leather skirt, a black Henley-neck T-shirt, and a black hoodie. Gustave just stood off to the side, looking nowhere in particular except occasionally at his wristwatch. Penelope leaned over to me and whispered, "Gustave is getting nervous. He has a cooking program that he likes to watch on Friday evenings."

I looked at Gustave from behind a pair of huge and expensive sunglasses I was trying on. "Him? He didn't seem like the cooking-channel type to me. I expected him to me more of the horror-channel type, you know, like the old black-and-white bore fests from the last century." We laughed again, and Penelope was particularly careful not to let Gustave know that he was the subject of our giggles.

"We really should go," she said.

I put everything back at the front counter and sauntered out of the store.

"KC," she said, "you're not buying any of those clothes?"

"Nah, half the fun of shopping is trying stuff on and waiting till you find something you really *must* have."

She laughed again and turned toward her butler. "Gustave, could you please take us home now?"

"Yes, miss." Gustave looked relieved.

On the ride home, we talked a little more. I learned how hard it was for Penelope to make friends because her Dad kept moving around. But the good news was that his position at the Ironwood Museum looked like it might be long-term, at least until she graduated from high school. That made her happy. Me too.

I tried to persuade her to wear something besides black. "You have such nice coloring. I think you could really look striking with some color in your wardrobe."

"Me, striking? I never thought of myself that way."

"Yeah, striking, you know, exotic. My friend Air thinks you're hot."

"The skateboard enthusiast?"

"Skateboarder . . . He probably wouldn't like being called an enthusiast."

We laughed again. She suddenly got serious. "He thinks I'm attractive?"

"A lot of boys do. You can see them looking at you as you're walking through the halls."

"Interesting. Your friend Air is kind of cute as well."

Suddenly my cheeks were burning. "I suppose he is. He asked me to the Halloween dance this Friday."

"A dance this Friday! That is Halloween!"

"Yes, it is."

Penelope leaned forward toward the driver's seat, suddenly very serious. "Gustave, please go a little faster. I must get back to Father's study!"

Chapter 13

Foote Problems

I 'VE NEVER REALLY thought of Mr. Foote as a nice guy. *Grumpy* or *grouchy* would probably be better words to describe him. And he seemed to dislike ninth-grade freshmen in particular. To make matters worse, Mr. Foote was really big and burly. Yes, that was our Mr. Foote—big, burly, and surly. And he was probably not afraid of anything except, possibly, ghosts.

"We have got to keep him away from school on Friday!" said Penelope. We were using the school library's study cubicle to plan our strategy.

"You can't be for real?"

"What?"

"I mean, you can't be serious. Foote will never stay away because a couple of ninth graders told him that a ghost is after him."

"I see what you mean. But I also think that he already knows something is haunting the basement. Maybe it would be easier to convince him than we think."

"I still doubt it. Foote won't listen to us. Besides, I've been talking to some of the tenth graders, and apparently, Foote supervises the setting up of the DJ and serves as a chaperone. He does this at all dances. That probably goes double for Halloween."

"Hmmm . . . ," said Penelope, "he certainly is committed."

"Yeah, he's got no life outside of school."

"Maybe because he knows that Richelieu High School is haunted. After all, he has been at the school as a custodian, and he's down there in the basement where the paranormal activity is highest. Maybe none of this is a new phenomenon."

"You mean, it's been going on for years?"

"That could very well be the case," Penelope said. "And Mr. Foote may very well be aware of it. That could explain why he has stayed on so far past retirement age."

"How do you know that?"

"Simple math . . . Sarah Jane died at the Halloween dance of her senior year. Mr. Foote, Mrs. Perault, and the others were all in the graduating class, 1958. That makes Mr. Foote sixty-eight or sixty-nine years old."

"Okay, so you're saying that Mr. Foote knows that the school is haunted, but he might not be aware that it's focused on him?"

"That sounds like a reasonable summary. And with that in mind, he might be open to listening to our warning to stay out of school the next few days."

"Okay, Penelope, but things don't work like that. We just can't walk up to him and say, 'Mr. Foote, you look tired. You're suffering from ghost-overload syndrome. Take a few days off.'"

Penelope smirked, "That was not exactly what I had in mind. Perhaps a detailed explanation of what we think is going on and why. We could type out our evidence and leave it in his office."

"That'll make for some entertaining reading . . . And FYI, if we're caught anywhere near the basement, we're in trouble, big time!"

"Not if we had an excuse to be there. Then it's just a case of getting our evidence to Mr. Foote as surreptitiously as possible."

"In English?"

Penelope sighed, "We've got to be sneaky."

"Oh, I can do sneaky."

*   *   *

Penelope had another study hall later that morning and composed a letter to Mr. Foote. She showed it to me at lunch.

"Penelope, I'm not sure if Mr. Foote is going to buy any of this."

"He does not have to buy it, just believe it."

I was skeptical. Just then, Air walked over from the skateboarders' table.

"Yo, KC, Penny . . . uh, Penelope. What's up?" I instantly stashed the note.

"Hey, Air. What's up with you?"

"Hello, Air," said Penelope. Was that a demure little purr in her voice, or was I imagining things?

Air must have noticed it too because he was suddenly a little nervous. He turned toward me, stammering slightly.

"Uh, KC, uh have you thought about what I was asking you last week?"

Suddenly I felt as if I was in the spotlight. I looked at Air, and I looked at Penelope, who had a very curious look on her face.

"Umm," I said, "no, I mean, yes . . . I mean, I'm still not sure. Some things have come up." I looked past Air at Penelope. Air caught that too.

"Things?" he replied with a slightly nauseous look on his face. "You mean like *things* or like 'things'?" He motioned quotation marks in the air.

"I don't really know what. I mean, can we talk about this later?"

"Yeah, later like later tonight or later like NEVER?"

"Tonight, Air, like later tonight."

Suddenly I was really feeling like he was getting in my face, so I picked up my lunch tray and backpack. "Catch you guys later. I gotta bounce."

As I dropped off my tray and crossed the cafeteria toward the hallway, I saw Air and Penelope sitting there. At first they looked really uncomfortable, then Penelope started talking to him in a very animated way. I thinking she was pouring on the charm. Suddenly I was mad at both of them. Ugh! I felt like screaming. I stomped right past them, not saying a word, and threw open the door into the hallway.

*   *   *

That night, Air called me. I was really reluctant to talk to him, but I did.

"So, KC, decided anything about the dance Friday night?" Boy, he sure got right to the point.

"Penelope and I were actually planning to do something that night."

"She told me that you guys would be there."

"She did?"

"Yeah, she said that you guys were going and I'd probably see you there."

"Well, I guess that she was hoping to go and meet people but kind of wanted me to hang with her for company. You know, it's got to be weird being foreign and in a new school."

"Word, I hear that. But I was kind of getting the idea that she was thinking of meeting some boy there."

"A boy? Who?"

"Well, she kept asking me stuff about Brett Henry."

Hmmm, I thought to myself, *the biggest up-and-coming jock in the school and our demure little foreign student already has her sights on him.*

"Can't be," I said. "Brett's a tenth grader, and besides, they have nothing in common."

"Remember today when you left us in the lunch room . . . Well, Brett was the numero uno topic of conversation. Whether they have anything in common or not, I think she wants to ask him out."

My head was swimming with information overload. Penelope's love life was the last thing I wanted to hear about, so I went back to topic.

"Air, we're friends, and this whole dance-slash-date thing is freaking me out. Maybe it's best we just keep it casual, and I'll catch you guys at the dance."

"Chill, KC. I understand. That would be cool."

"Cool, see you tomorrow."

"Tomorrow."

Well, that was easy. I guess that was one of the best things about Air. Even when things got complicated, they were easy to straighten out. Then I started to wonder about Penelope. What was she up to talking to Air about Brett Henry? And why did she tell Air that we'd see him at the dance? Air was my friend, not hers. Was she going way over the line? I couldn't quite figure out why, but Penelope had this weird ability to get me really aggravated really fast.

"ARGHHHH!" I screamed into my pillow.

Suddenly I looked toward the open door of my room. My little brother was standing there in pajamas covered in pictures of his favorite cartoon characters.

"Mom," he yelled, "KC's screaming into her pillow again!"

"Who are you, squirt, the pillow police?"

James stepped up to me, his head barely reaching my chin, and looked up at me in wide-eyed innocence that quickly turned into a defiant little snarl. "No!" he said. "I'm the big sister with attitude police!"

I pretended to get angry and took the pillow in both hands, waving it wildly over my head. "Why, you little . . . ," I said and chased him down the top floor, landing to his room. I caught up with him and planted the pillow on his head with a resounding *thump*.

James crumpled to the ground as if he was mortally wounded, and I jumped on top of him. This would call for a major tickle attack, and he knew it. He was screaming even before I touched him. As I started tickling him on his ribs, he was kicking his legs wildly on the floor. Suddenly from below, the call of the Wild Mom came vibrating up the staircase and through the floorboards.

"KIDS, GO TO BED, *NOW!*"

When my mother yelled that loudly, it meant that we had to do whatever she was asking or face the consequences.

I messed up James's hair. "Good night, squirt."

James was still ready to wrestle. "You got off easy this time, girl."

"WHAT-ever. Good night."

As I went to sleep, I pondered the problem of getting our message to Mr. Foote. The problem was that Penelope and I needed a reason to be out of our class and in the hallway. School authorities were already keeping an eye on us because we were nearby during both "unusual" events. I was sure that Mr. Cortez actually thought we were the culprits even though he never sent any notes home. So getting to Mr. Foote's custodial office in the basement would be a major obstacle.

Sometime between 3:00 and 5:00 a.m., I came up with a plan for delivering our warning to Mr. Foote. This was Tuesday, and we only had four days to warn him to stay away. When I got to school, I frantically searched for Penelope. I caught her just as she was going into homeroom.

"Penelope, I know how we can get your note to Mr. Foote *surreptitiously.*"

"Yes . . . ?"

"Yes, and all you've got to do is take a fall off the balance beam."

Chapter 14

Off Balance

THE PLAN WAS really simple. Penelope would tell our PE teacher, Mrs. Crawford, that she thought it over and she would like to join the gymnastics team. With Penelope's gymnastic skills, Mrs. Crawford would jump at the chance to get her in the team. Then Penelope would have to convince her that I've been working with her and that she really needs me as a spotter. Then she would fake a fall, and I would bring her down to the nurse's office, which just happened to be right next to Mr. Foote's office in the dreaded lower floor of the school. It was a simple plan. Believable. A piece of cake.

The only problem was that Mrs. Crawford wasn't buying it.

"Watson," she said, "you're telling me that you're interested in gymnastics?"

"Yes, Mrs. Crawford. I started showing Penelope the school, and she showed me some of her moves. So we decided that if I was her spotter . . . uh . . ."

Penelope chimed in, "We thought that I would try to teach KC some of the basics I learned in Czechoslovakia while I would get a spotter who will know my routine."

Mrs. Crawford stroked her chin. "Hmmm, makes sense, I guess. And I suppose that anything that would get Watson here interested in sports is okay with me. We were going to start basketball today, and as you can see, the balance beam and the mats are still set up in the other section of the gym. So you two could go through some warm-ups while I get the rest of the class set up."

I was amazed at how cooperative Mrs. Crawford was being. She obviously really wanted Penelope in the gymnastics team. Cha-ching! Things were working out good so far. We crossed the gym and slipped off our flip-flops, stepping onto the large rubbery blue mats.

"Okay, sneaky one," said Penelope, "now what do we do?"

"Stretch, warm up, show me a move or two?"

"Can you do any gymnastics?" she asked.

"Cartwheel, a really lame cartwheel . . . Sorry."

"Let's just stretch and warm up, then I'll try some routines on the beam. On my third pass, I will dismount and pretend I have injured myself. I'll make a big noise."

"And you call me sneaky one," I said. "I'll have to keep my eyes on you."

"Yes, you will. You will be my spotter, yes?"

"No, I mean, yes. I mean, I'll spot you but just don't overact. Teachers are notorious for spotting a scam."

"I won't sweat."

"I think you mean *no sweat*."

Penelope and I warmed up for about ten minutes, and then she mounted the balance beam. She started with something like a slow-motion roundoff. She placed her hands on the beam then slowly, with perfect balance, brought her feet over her body onto the beam. She did two passes, and then she suddenly exploded into the same handsprings I'd seen her perform on the second day of school. When she got to the opposite end of the balance beam, she pushed off, brought her legs into a landing position. Just as her feet hit the floor, she gave out a cry and fell back.

"Penelope!" I yelled, half believing that she was hurt.

Mrs. Crawford sprinted across the gym. "My gosh, what happened! KC, I thought you were spotting?"

"It was not KC's fault, Mrs. Crawford. My dismount was poor, and I landed on my weak ankle."

"Penelope, you should have wrapped that for support! You know better! It doesn't look like anything worse than a sprain, hasn't even started to swell, but you'd better get down to the nurse's office and get some ice on that right away! KC, help her."

It couldn't have worked better.

The minute we were outside of the gym, Penelope stopped leaning on me. "Now as long as our luck continues and Mr. Foote is not in his office . . ." She let that thought trail off as we walked toward the far stairwell that led to the lower level and to the office of Ms. Hartigay, the school nurse. Actually, this was her temporary office. The real one was getting a makeover, and the only available space was in the basement. In the middle of all the creepy sounds and other weird stuff, they had moved Ms. Hartigay's office to the basement. She couldn't have been happy about it.

Just as we stepped off the stair into the murkiness of the long, dark corridor, that creepy service guy, Mr. DuLac, came walking down the hall toward us, wheeling some kind of utility cart in front of him. At first, all I could see was his hunched figure lit from behind by the red light of an old-fashioned Exit sign. He didn't say a word; he just glanced over at us from under his thick, bushy eyebrows and wheeled off into the gloom.

We rounded the corner and went right to Mr. Foote's office. Penelope put her ear to the door and listened. Hearing nothing, she knocked gently. No response. She turned the doorknob and opened the door. The office was small and dingy. The gray steel desk filled most of the space. Spiderwebs and old rusty pipes decorated the walls. On the desk was a phone, a large calendar, and a chipped coffee cup containing pencils of different lengths. On the opposite wall were several charts marked with Mr. Foote's unreadable scrawl.

I stood at the threshold watching the hall. "Penelope! Come on. Leave the note and let's bounce before someone comes."

I jumped when I heard the voice of Mr. Foote coming from around the corner of the hallway. He was talking to someone on his walkie-talkie. Weird things were happening all over the school in the last couple of weeks. Pipes were breaking; mirrors in the girls' lavatory were dropping off the walls. It was keeping him and his small custodial staff pretty busy.

I turned back to Penelope and, in a panic, whispered, "Mr. Foote is coming back. We've got to go NOW! Wait, someone else is coming." I heard the squeak of a wheel and then the familiar accent of Mr. DuLac.

"Ah, Mr. Foote. I am replacing all the batteries on the surveillance cameras. They are being tripped off a lot, yes? After the school closes, they are being very activated . . ." His voice lowered, but I could hear them continue to talk in muffled tones.

"Okay, Mr. Foote and Mr. DuLac are talking. Leave the note and let's go!"

"I'm just trying to find a spot where he won't miss my note."

"How about the top of his DESK, duh?"

"Yes, that should work, but his desk is a mess."

"Just leave it!" I pleaded.

Thankfully, she stepped back into the hall and quietly closed the door behind her.

"Okay, it is done. Let's go."

We continued on to the nurse's office. Ms. Hartigay was always pleasant and upbeat. I think that she was glad to have some company. She looked at

Penelope's ankle. "Nothing broken," she declared. But let's put some ice on it to make sure it doesn't swell up. KC, you can go back to class. I'll keep Penelope here for a few more minutes."

"Do I need a note or something?"

"I'll send a note back with Penelope."

I left and walked quickly toward the stairwell. I didn't want to be down there any longer than I had to. There was no sign of Mr. Foote or Mr. DuLac in the hallway. As I passed Mr. Foote's office, I glanced sideways into the open doorway. He was sitting at his desk with the note crumpled in his hand. He was turned toward the doorway, staring up at the corner of his office that was hidden from view. His face was a ghastly white, and his entire body trembled. I stood there just watching him. I was in plain sight, but it was as if he didn't see me. I slowly approached the threshold of his office. He continued to stare, and slowly I began to understand that the expression on his face was one of *terror*. The hair on my neck stood up as a chill passed over my body. I slowly backed away. I couldn't help myself. "M-Mr. Foote," I said in a voice choked by fright. "Mr. Foote, what is it? Are you all right?"

Then slowly he turned toward me and blinked as if he was coming out of a dream. "No," he said, "it can't be! No, no!"

Then without warning, he was up on his feet and bolting down the hall—at least what passed for bolting for a guy of his age and size. I was left standing in that gloomy hall, staring at his receding figure. Then I heard a moan that seemed to come from everywhere. I was trembling, but without thinking, I turned toward his office door. Framed by the doorway to Mr. Foote's office was the gray misty figure of a girl. She was dressed in a gown. I could clearly see the large skirt adorned with tassels and ribbons. Her hair and her garments floated around her as if she was underwater. My heart pounded, but I couldn't turn away. Then her blurry face seemed twist into a mask of outrage. Her mouth was contorted in a soundless scream. Then the office door slammed, and I was struck with a force that threw me against the lockers on the opposite hall of the corridor. My legs became weak, and I crumpled to the hard granite floor.

Chapter 15

Meltdown

WHEN I CAME around, the school nurse was putting something horrible smelling under my nose. Penelope was standing next to her. So was a trembling Mr. Foote. Principal Cortez and Mr. DuLac completed the group.

"I don't know what's going on around here," said Mr. Cortez. "But I intend to find out! Everyone to my office . . . NOW!"

"Me too!" said Ms. Hartigay. "This basement is giving me the creeps!"

Mr. Cortez just nodded his head, and we all marched up to his office.

Penelope and I were told to sit in the office waiting room while he spoke to Mr. Foote, Ms. Hartigay, and Mr. DuLac.

I couldn't hear very much of the conversation, but occasionally, the rumble of Mr. Cortez's deep baritone voice shook the door and the opaque glass wall of his office. When the door of his office finally opened, I jumped.

The three adults filed past us, looking straight ahead.

"Ms. Watson, Ms. Dredalus," boomed Mr. Cortez, "I'll see you both now."

We both got up and marched single file into his office.

"Sit down, please."

We sat in the two chairs facing his desk. Mr. Cortez sat looking at his desk with his hands clasped in front of him. I noticed a little vein pulsing on his temple, and his jaw muscles were clenching and unclenching. He was really mad. After a minute of silence, he cleared his throat.

"Give me one reason why I shouldn't suspend the both of you right now?!" My jaw dropped. He was talking suspension. I had a lump in my throat, and I started to feel dizzy.

But Penelope stayed calm and leveled her eyes at the principal. "With all due respect, Mr. Cortez, you shouldn't suspend us because we did not do anything wrong."

"Didn't do anything wrong! You both left a class under false pretenses just so you could play that prank on Mr. Foote."

"I'm sorry, sir, but we played no prank."

"What about this note?"

"We were concerned for Mr. Foote's safety."

"Safety from what, your Halloween pranks? This has been going on for almost the entire semester, and I've had enough! Lockers slamming, strange sounds, things breaking, horrible odors, students getting scared half out of their wits by 'strange apparitions.' Nonsense! And almost every time something odd has occurred, you two are nearby! You are both suspended!"

I broke down. "Mr. Cortez, please, my mother will kill me!"

"You should have thought of that before you started these shenanigans."

"Mr. Cortez," said Penelope, "KC had nothing to do with this. Please do not suspend her."

"Aha! So you admit that you were responsible for this prank!"

"No, I'm only responsible for getting KC involved in this."

"In your elaborate *Halloween prank*!"

Mr. Cortez stood there with his hands on his hips. I sank back into my chair. I was dead. suspended and dead. My mother would ground me until I was twenty-one.

Just then, there was a gentle knock on the door. Before Mr. Cortez could answer, Mr. Foote peeked around the half-opened door. "Mr. Cortez, can I speak with you?"

"Now, Elliot? I'm just about to suspend these two pranksters."

"I know, and I think you'd be making a big mistake."

"But you said that these two scared you out of your wits!"

"No, I said what I saw scared me . . . right after I read their note . . . But believe me, what I saw was no teenage prank . . . It couldn't have been. What I saw was *real*!"

"Elliot, come on. You can't be serious."

"I am . . . completely serious . . . I saw something, but it was no trick."

"I would have to agree." It was Mr. DuLac, standing in the doorway with a laptop in his hand. "What Mr. Foote saw was no prank!"

Mr. Cortez sank back against his desk. He ran his fingers through his graying hair. "Is this entire school going crazy? What are you both talking about?"

Mr. DuLac placed the laptop on the principal's desk and fingered the touch pad until a video window appeared on the screen.

"As you know, I have these little digital surveillance cameras all over the school. I just had to retrieve the chip from the camera I have positioned near Mr. Foote's office. I looked it over very quickly. I have the footage from twenty minutes ago when the so-called prank occurred . . . Would you care to see it, Principal Cortez?"

"Will it finally clear up this mess?"

"Perhaps."

Mr. Cortez let out a long sigh. "All right, let's see what you have."

Mr. DuLac double-clicked on the window, and the video started to play. We all crowded around the laptop for a better look. On the screen, we could see the hallway and Mr. Foot's office viewed from a high angle. The image was gray and smeared. I saw myself walk into the scene. We saw Mr. Foote bolt from his office, and there I was, gawking at his office door. Then very faintly there was something in the doorway. Something indistinct that distorted whatever was behind it. I saw myself stagger back and then crash into the lockers, pushed by an invisible force. Before the door slammed shut, there was the image of a girl in a dress in the doorway. Mr. DuLac quickly clicked on the Pause icon. "Whatever this is," he said, "this is what scared Mr. Foote and caused this young lady to faint."

Mr. Cortez turned toward Mr. DuLac. "Are you telling me that this is some kind of gho—"

Mr. DuLac threw up his hand. "I never use that term . . . I prefer *paranormal phenomenon*."

"What? You prefer? Who exactly are you, Mr. DuLac? Seems you have more of an interest here than security cameras."

Suddenly Mr. DuLac straightened up to his full height. He reached up to his face and removed the bushy mustache and shaggy wig to reveal a tall black-haired man with fine aristocratic features. He crossed the room and stood next to Penelope. "I am Dr. Mikhail Dredalus of the Ironwood Museum of Antiquities and Penelope's father. I am also an expert on the paranormal."

Mr. Cortez and Mr. Foote both stared at Mr. DuLac, I mean, Mr. Dredalus for a long time. I wasn't sure what part of the last few minutes they were processing, but they were both dumbfounded.

Finally, Mr. Cortez spoke. "Do you mean to tell me that you came into this school under false pretenses to set up your surveillance equipment? I should have you arrested!"

"Sir, that's your prerogative, but I assure you my credentials are flawless, and I did provide the services you contracted me for and just as you specified. I positioned the cameras where you requested and monitored all the recordings for anything 'out of the ordinary.' Here are the results of that service . . . And my professional opinion is that Richelieu Central School very probably is haunted."

Mr. Cortez shot up like a bolt and slammed his opened hand on his desk. "Preposterous! Outrageous! I want you out of school property immediately!"

Mr. Foote threw up his hands. "Gentlemen, please! This isn't getting us anywhere!" He turned to Mr. Cortez. "Luis, I think Mr. DuLa . . . uh, Mr. Dredalus is right. I think the school is haunted, and I think I know why."

"Well, okay, Elliot," said Mr. Cortez, throwing up his hands. "If you can shed some light on this, please do."

Grumpy old Mr. Foote suddenly looked so sad. "I don't think it's a good idea to have students present."

"Girls," said Mr. Cortez, "you can go. Ask Mrs. Costanzia to give you a pass to the gym. You'll have just enough time to change before the last bell. Oh, and for now, until I have all the facts, your suspension is, um . . . *suspended.*"

Without saying another word, I ushered Penelope out the door before our principal changed his mind. Minutes later on the way to the girls' locker room, Penelope grabbed my arm.

"This is terrible. We should have been allowed to stay!"

"What? Are you crazy? We're not going to get suspended. That's good enough for me."

"Not for me! KC, nothing has changed . . . Whatever this paranormal event is, it's still going on, building in intensity. All my devices confirm this."

"Well, can't you ask your father? He's in on the meeting. He can tell you what Mr. Foote said when he gets home."

"If Mr. Foote asks him to keep everything confidential, then he'll keep everything to himself. He is a very honorable and honest man, and if he gives his word that he'll keep something confidential, then it's as good as done."

"Well, that stinks! Oh, and by the way, that wasn't too cool, not telling me that creepy Mr. DuLac was your dad."

"Besides," she continued, ignoring my comment, "knowing the cause of these events is just half the problem. The real problem is how to stop this haunting."

I just looked at her and said, "That is if we *can* stop it."

Chapter 16

Friday

BY FRIDAY, THE weather had turned bad. Thick gray clouds choked the sky, bringing a constant dreary rain. Even by noon, it looked like early evening.

Thursday night I got an e-mail from Penelope, describing how Mr. Foote had given Mr. Cortez and Dr. Dredalus a vague background story of the events leading to Sarah Jane McCormack's drowning. Penelope had already pieced together most of it from the microfiches at the library and from Mrs. Perault.

According to Penelope, some of the more popular kids wanted to play a prank on Sarah Jane. They lured her into the indoor swimming pool and locked her in just to scare her. But according to Mr. Foote, the sliding floor was always over the swimming pool and it was safe. Sarah Jane, somehow, had managed to throw the switch that caused the floor to retract, dropping her into the pool in the dark. She must have panicked and eventually drowned. Mr. Foote didn't reveal how they got her down there or how he knew so much about the details, but he did say that he had nothing to do with the prank. But there was some kind of Halloween prank that brought Sarah Jane into that deadly situation, and in some way, Elliot Foote was directly or indirectly involved. We sent IMs back and forth for a while, trying to fill in the missing pieces, but we were stumped. We TTYLed around ten.

Penelope wasn't in homeroom the next morning and didn't show up until math class. She was all business, dressed in her cat-girl, ninja-warrior getup. After class, I went up to her.

"What's up?"

"Up? Nothing's up. In fact, everything is down. Don't you feel it?"

"Yeah, I do. It's like everything is moving slow like we're all moving through syrup."

"A good description. It is a field of ectoplasmic energy."

"Say what?"

"I believe that Sarah Jane is gathering energy from everyone in the school . . . Teenagers are a great source of psychic energy. The theory is that spirits form out of a substance called ectoplasm. But it takes energy to do it. In order to manifest themselves, spirits must gather energy. It's one of the reasons that we see temperature readings drop when ghosts appear. This is the 'entity' gathering energy from every available source, even the air temperature. My EM readings are off the charts, and there are cold spots everywhere."

"Okay. But what does it all mean?"

"As you would say, it means that Sarah Jane is getting ready to 'party.'"

"That doesn't sound good."

Penelope got real serious and looked at me with an intense look on her face.

"I don't know what's going to happen, but I think it will happen tonight at the dance. In fact, I'm sure of it. This is the fiftieth anniversary of her death. I can sense her. I can sense her anger building along with her strength."

"Penelope, you're scaring me."

"Sarah Jane is scaring me. I can't explain it, but I just know that she's close by and getting ready. The best case is that she fully manifests and scares the daylights out of everyone."

"What's the worse case?"

"Unlike a lot of spirits, Sarah Jane manifests like a poltergeist . . . This means lots of telekinetic manifestations."

"ENGLISH, please!"

"Moving things, breaking things. Not good."

"So what's the plan?"

"Simple, really. Go to the dance and keep our eyes open . . . And if it gets too dangerous, *run*."

"Some plan."

The rest of the school day dragged on. I had butterflies in my stomach. Penelope was distant, distracted. We passed into each other in the hall, and she didn't even seem to recognize me.

But it got weirder. After lunch, I was up on the second floor, and there she was flirting with Brett Henry at his locker even to the point where she was holding his arm as they went walking down the hall. And there was

Brett looking both a little proud and a little perplexed with this cute ninth grader hanging all over him. It just didn't seem like the Penelope I knew. So being the impulsive person I am, I started to walk up to them. She looked right at me, and I swear Penelope didn't recognize me! They just passed me by while I stood there gawking. Oh my gosh, sometimes she could be sooo weird. I mean, it's the evening of the big ghost-thingy whatchamacallit and she's flirting with a tenth grader!

By the time the last bell rang, I was way ready to leave. Riding home on the bus, I kept wondering if I should warn Air about what might be going on tonight. I could freak him out, or he might just think that I was crazy, so I just kept quiet. The bus pulled up to the corner of Whitney and Battle, and we both got off.

"Still going tonight?"

"Yeah, you?"

"I'll be there."

"Cool."

"How about Penny Dreadful?" He nodded toward Penelope's house.

"'S far as I know."

"Did she ask Brett Henry to the dance?"

"What? Why do you ask?"

"Well, I saw her talking to him a few times today. They were looking pretty friendly."

"I saw them too. But I really don't know. She doesn't tell me *everything*, you know."

"No? I thought girls shared all that kind of stuff."

"Not really . . . But with all of today's *drama*, who knows? Brett might be joining Penny Dreadful tonight." I was suddenly fuming at her. I wasn't jealous or anything, but I thought we were friends and she would let me know what was happening.

"Ha, I got you doing it too . . . The name kind of applies, right?"

"I guess . . . Hey, I got to go."

"'Okay, later."

"Later." I shrugged to myself. Air looked a little hurt, but right then, I wasn't in the mood for any more drama or gossip.

The dance started at 7:30, but usually, only committee members, preppies, and the hopelessly nerdified were there before 7:45. So I had some time to chill. After dinner, I went upstairs and went through the usual frustrating routine of trying to find something to wear. I finally settled on black jeans, an orange top (my mother insisted that I wear *something* that looked like Halloween), and a black hoodie with a glitter design printed on it. I accessorized with a bunch of bangles, a necklace that my old friend Margaret had made me last summer, and a pair of long dangling earrings. I completed the outfit with my black high-tops. I got the Mom Seal of Approval. Dad offered to drive me, which was cool with me. That would be one less lecture I'd have to listen to from Mom. As we got in, Frisket jumped into the car.

"Have fun, honey," Mom called from the kitchen. "Yeah, have fun, honey," parroted James in an annoyingly whiny voice. "Don't kiss any boys!"

"Mom!"

"I'll take care of your brother . . . Just have fun."

As Dad and I drove down Battle Avenue toward the school, he turned to me "So, Kat [Dad's the only one who calls me Kat], this is officially your first high school dance." I had actually forgotten that all-too-important fact. "No date?"

I was embarrassed. "No, Dad, not officially. I'm meeting Air and some other friends there."

"Oh, Air, huh?"

"Is that a problem?"

"No, no problem. Air seems like a good kid . . . And I know where he lives." Then he laughed at his lame joke.

"I'll be fine, Dad."

"I know you will, *KC*."

As we drove up to the school, Penelope's black Mercedes was pulling away. Penelope was standing near the curb.

"Hey, isn't that your friend?" asked my father.

"Uh-huh."

"Well, good. You've got some company." He honked the horn twice. Penelope stopped and turned toward us.

As we pulled to the curb, Frisket jumped into the backseat and started to whimper.

"Hey, boy," I said. "What's the matter? It's like he's scared or something."

"Maybe he doesn't like school either, or maybe he's not into that whole goth thing." Dad chuckled, nodding toward Penelope.

I looked up at Penelope waiting by the curb. She was dressed in a black-on-black ensemble made of a wispy top with long sleeves made of a lacy fabric. The multilayered black skirt was made of the same wispy fabric cut in an uneven hemline. Beneath her skirt, she wore black leggings and black boots. She wore a silver bracelet and necklace. Her square-cut hair was perfectly combed, framing her face. She was pale, and she wore dark eye shadow that made her look posilutely stark and very gothic.

"Well, got to go, Dad. The dance is over at ten thirty."

"I'll be here."

"Later. Love ya." I got out of the car and went over to Penelope.

"Your father?"

"Yup."

"Looks like a nice man."

"He's cool . . . most of the time."

"Ready to go in?"

"Ready, setty, go!" I was trying to be upbeat. Penelope was about as deadpan as I'd ever seen her. She just turned and started into the annual Richelieu High School Halloween dance.

Chapter 17

Friday—Part Deux

I HAD TO hand it to the decorating committee; they did a great job on the school. The hallway leading to the gym had several fog machines that carpeted the corridor with a thick gray mist. Weirdly twisted papier-mâché trees seemed to be growing out of the mist. Giant rubber bats and fuzzy toy spiders nested in the gnarled branches. Of course, there were fake cobwebs everywhere.

Placed along the hall were several life-size dummies decorated as a vampire, a mummy, and some gory creation I couldn't identify. The dummies were bathed in red or green light projected from floodlights placed at their feet. Loud music from the gym seeped out into the hallway.

At the door to the gym, two students were seated at a folding table. They both looked like juniors or maybe seniors. The girl was dressed as a vampire with a long black wig streaked with silver and was in a black gothic-looking dress. She had white makeup on her face, way too heavy eye shadow, and liner. Her lips were vivid red with a trickle of stage blood "dripping" from the corner of her mouth. I guess she thought she was *all that* because she totally ignored us. The boy was a ghoul. He was friendlier. He wore a tattered black suit, gray face paint with cheeks and temples blackened slightly to give him a gaunt look. He had horrid yellow fake teeth in his mouth that made him hard to understand.

"Tickesh preaze," said the ghoul.

"We don't have tickets."

"Y' go to thish schoo?"

"Yeah."

"Three dollarsh each."

We paid the admission and entered the gym. We stepped through the gym doors and were hit with the deafening sound of the DJ's speakers. Spotlights of red, orange, and green lit the gym. There were also black lights placed in the darkest corners of the huge room, throwing out pools of weird purple light. More fake spiderwebs and orange and black streamers hung from every available spot. Off to one side of the gym, some art students had created a huge cutout of a castle in silhouette. The cutout was made of several sheets of plywood cut in the shape of turrets and spires. The cutout windows of the castle were filled with eerie amber lights. Students were lining up to have their photos taken with some student disguised as Frankenstein's monster.

Richelieu was an old school. The gym doubled as an auditorium. On the stage, the DJ stood at a turntable framed by two huge columns of speakers. His headphones were perched at an odd angle over his baseball cap. He swayed to the beat as he was throwing down loops and scratching over them, weaving a thumping fabric of sound. Strobe lights pulsed to the beat of the music.

The rest of the gym was basically one big dance floor. Students were dancing all around us. I sighed to myself, wishing that I were only here to enjoy the party and not as part of Penny Dreadful's ghost-hunting drama.

I scanned the room for Air and his friends, but I didn't see him anywhere.

I turned to Penelope and yelled over the music, "Now what?"

"I don't know. This is my first American high school dance . . . Don't you know?"

"It's my first too, but I was talking about the whole, you know, situation."

"Oh yes . . . We wait for something to happen, try to act casual . . . And if some cute boy asks us to dance—"

"You mean like Brett Henry?"

"Excuse me? Who is Brett Henry?"

Penelope was sure acting weird.

"You know, the guy you've been flirting with all day and for the past week."

"KC, honestly, I don't know what you mean . . . Who is this boy?"

"Well, you tossed a blazing cell phone at him on the second day of school."

"What? Oh, that boy . . . I haven't spoken to him since."

I didn't know what to think. Was she lying? Messing with me? There was more to this girl than met the eye. I decided to just let it go.

"Let's go get some punch."

We zigzagged around the dancing couples and stood in front of a long table covered with stacks and stacks of clear plastic cups surrounding a huge punch bowl filled with some mysterious dark red concoction. Someone had already ladled the punch into some of the cups. Mr. Foote was doing guard duty over the punch bowl. He nodded to us as we approached. We both got ourselves a plastic cup filled with punch and sat down on the extended bleachers. Students were arriving constantly, and the gym was getting really crowded. I saw Air walking toward us.

"Hey yo, KC, uh, hi, Penelope."

"Hello, Air." said Penelope. I just waved. "Hey."

Air thrust his hands into his back pockets and looked around the gym. "Whoa, pretty sick what they did to the gym."

"Yeah," I said, "totally off the chain."

"Yeah, totally."

We both looked at Penelope to include her in the conversation. She looked back at us, a little puzzled, and then realized we were looking for a response.

"Totally," she said.

"Uh, look, KC, a bunch of me and my buds are here, not too sure if we'll hang all night . . . How 'bout that dance?" Arrrgh, he sure wasn't wasting any time. I looked at Penelope.

"Don't worry about me. I'm fine."

"Okay . . . See ya." I jumped down off the bleachers. She sure didn't seem fine. I was glad to get away from Penelope because she was acting so weird.

Air and I started dancing, and that was weird too. I'd never actually seen him dance before; I was beginning to think that he should stick to the skateboard.

"I'm glad we could meet up, KC, at least for a dance."

"Me too!" I shouted back over the music.

"What's with your BFF tonight? She seems out of it."

"Not sure . . . Maybe she's distracted."

"Whoa," said Air, pointing over my shoulder. "I guess she *is*." I turned toward the direction his finger was pointing and OMG! I almost fell to the floor.

There was Brett Henry sitting next to Penelope. And Penelope was sitting there really pouring on the charm. She was smiling coyly at him, batting her eyelids. It was almost *gross*!

I turned back to Air. "This is whack! Five minutes ago she told me that she didn't even remember him . . . Now look at her."

"I don't get this girl stuff . . . You're all confusing to me."

"Air, this is more than just 'girl stuff.' This is way psycho!"

Just then, the lights went out. Some students hooted and hollered, thinking that this was part of the festivities; others screamed. The emergency lights came on, blinding me for a second. When my eyes adjusted to the lights, I was astounded to see Brett and Penelope dancing in the middle of the gym floor. Penelope had a firm grip on Brett's hands. I thought I saw Brett grimace. Penelope's face was like a mask—cold, expressionless. And her eyes—even from where I was standing, I could see that her eyes were no longer tawny gold but a cold, piercing *blue*!

"Air! Come on. Something's wrong . . . *really wrong*!" I grabbed Air by the hand and started pulling him toward Penelope and Brett.

Penelope saw us coming toward her and wheeled around to face us, knocking Brett off his feet as she held her grip on him.

"Penelope," I screamed, "what's wrong?"

Her face twisted into a mask of rage, and she yelled back in a booming voice, "Stay back!"

Air and I were thrown back as something unseen slammed into us. We lost our balance and slid across the polished gym floor.

I looked around at the astounded faces of the other students. Mr. Foote stood by the punch bowl, motionless. I saw the Frankenstein monster pull at his mask to reveal a very sweaty Dr. Dredalus, his black hair plastered to his forehead. He ran over to us.

"Come on. You've got to help me stop her! We've got to get her out of this building."

"But why?" I said. "What's happening? I don't understand."

"I think my daughter is possessed! Come on!"

We only moved a step or two when a tremendous shower of sparks came out of the DJ's stacked speakers. He staggered back as a second shower of sparks poured out of his amplifier and turntables. He was unhurt, and then he got up and ran off the stage and out of the gymnasium.

That was all that the other students needed to see, and then they all went hysterical! They all made a mad dash for the heavy gym doors. Dr. Dredalus ran over to the frozen Mr. Foote and dragged him over to where we were standing. One by one the emergency lights were exploding in showers of sparks, and the huge room was bathed in a weird glow. The lights were very dim and wavered like embers on the verge of igniting. There was a low humming sound filling the air.

"She's drawing from every available power source she can," cried Dr. Dredalus.

"What? Your daughter? Why?"

BOB BERRY

In front of me in the center of that abyss was Penelope, holding a terrified Brett Henry by one arm. They just seemed to be floating there.

Dr. Dredalus turned toward Mr. Foote, exasperated. "No, not my daughter . . . Sarah Jane McCormack." Mr. Foote just stood there, unable to understand what was happening. Dr. Dredalus shook the custodian. "We've got to get my daughter out of this building!" Penelope's dad released Mr. Foote and hurled himself toward his daughter. He was sent sprawling across the floor. Penelope started backing out of the gym with Brett Henry still in her grip. Brett was tall and strong but no match to her supernatural strength. I started toward her, hoping that somehow I could break through and stop this. Penelope was backing out of the gym with Brett in tow. I was stopped dead; something held me in place. I could hear Dr. Dredalus approaching us, and then Penelope screamed another ear-shattering "Stay back!"

Dr. Dredalus flew backward like a paper doll in a strong wind. I could feel the air around me turn deathly cold. The floor in front of me started to rise upward as if a huge mound was being thrust up from underneath the floor, then the floor fell away beneath me! It seemed that, for an instant, I was suspended there over a huge gaping black hole in the gym floor. The heels of my sneakers were barely gripping the edge. In front of me in the center of that abyss was Penelope, holding a terrified Brett Henry by one arm. They just seemed to be floating there. I had this sick feeling in my stomach as I began to teeter. Then I was falling! Something crashed into me from behind, and then I was tumbling across the gym floor away from the edge of the hole.

Before my mind could make any sense of what had happened, Air was pulling me to my feet and hugging me.

"KC, are you okay?"

"But I was falling . . ."

"I jumped and caught you just as you were going . . . I finally got some air when it really mattered!"

"But Penelope and Brett . . . ?"

Air turned me toward the wide circle of space. "Check that!" he said.

We peered over the edge carefully. Brett and Penelope were slowly floating down into the darkness as if they were on wires. Below them were a faint gray glow and a huge expanse of blue-gray concrete.

"The abandoned swimming pool! This is not good!" I said. "What can we do?" I looked around for someone to answer, but the only people left in the gym were Mr. Foote, Dr. Dredalus, Air, and myself.

Penelope's dad suddenly snapped into action, gesturing the rest of us toward the gym doors.

"We've got to get down there. Come, there is no time to lose!"

We started running toward the stairs, but Mr. Foote was barely able to keep up.

"I'm too old. I can't do this!"

"But you must! The lives of my daughter and that boy, your nephew, depend upon it!"

"The service elevator! Let's take that down!"

Mr. Foote trotted over to a gray metal door set back in an alcove. He inserted an odd-looking key in a wall panel, and the door opened, revealing an old elevator. We rushed into the car, and he pushed a button, sending us toward the basement. We stepped out of the elevator just opposite of Mr. Foote's small office.

"This way." He waved. "The entrance to the pool was over here."

We went a few more steps down the hall and came to a doorway walled up with bricks.

"We'll never get through that!" He sagged against a locker.

Dr. Dredalus grabbed him by the shoulders. "We've got to try! You have tools . . . a sledgeham—"

"Look!" I screamed out.

The bricks in the doorway were starting to move outward. One by one they were being pushed from behind and falling to the floor. And with every falling brick, a heavy door of rusting metal was being uncovered. When all the bricks were gone, there was terrible screeching sound of metal against metal, and slowly the door slid opened, spilling a greenish light into the hallway.

Penelope's dad walked over to the door and turned toward us. "I think we're being invited in."

Chapter 18

Pool Party

W E ALL STOOD there frozen in our tracks except Dr. Dredalus, who was already pushing the heavy door open.

I turned to Air. "You don't have to go in there. You were never part of this . . ."

"KC, we've been buds since kindergarten. No way I'm bailing now."

I guess I found some courage in Air's words. I took his hand, and I grabbed Mr. Foote's jacket sleeve and started guiding them both toward the door. I wasn't a quitter either, and now I knew that Penelope was in trouble, and I had to help her in any way I could.

Soon, we were standing in the huge abandoned pool area. The far corners were lost in the shadows. The only light was that strange grayish green glow that came from nowhere and everywhere. Then the door we had just entered through slammed shut with a sickening sound. We were stunned, and there was no sign of Dr. Dredalus, Penelope, or Brett.

"Why do I feel like a fly in a spiderweb? And where's Dr. Dredalus?" I asked.

Air ran to the pool's edge. "There, look, down in the pool."

We raced over to the pool's edge and looked down. The faded stenciled numbers on the pool wall indicated that this end of the pool was fifteen feet deep. I could see where a diving board tower had been anchored to the floor. Dr. Dredalus was already down on the bottom of the pool, trying to revive Penelope. Brett was lying unconscious beside Penelope. I suddenly became sick to my stomach at the thought that they might have fallen. "Are they . . . ?"

"They are both fine. They did not fall. But I will need you to help me bring them up!"

Penelope was instantly on her feet. Her father stumbled back across the pool floor as if he were pushed. She stood up and glared at us. "NO! He stays here!" she said, pointing to Brett Henry. Her voice was strange, almost as if it wasn't coming from her body. "He stays here until Elliot comes!"

Air and I turned toward Mr. Foote. He was pale and looking as if he was about to keel over. "No . . . I can't," he said faintly.

Dr. Dredalus scurried up the pool ladder; his head peeked up over the pool rim. "Mr. Foote! You must do as she asks . . . This is Sarah Jane speaking to you, *not my daughter!*"

"I know that . . . But what does she want from me? I had nothing to do with her de—with the accident!"

Dr. Dredalus crossed over to Mr. Foote, grabbing him by the sleeves of his jacket. "Mr. Foote, there is something she wants from you that will put her to rest and end this."

Mr. Foote was paralyzed. Frustrated, Penelope's dad slid back down the ladder. Penelope was just standing there, rigid like a statue. Brett was groaning, starting to come around.

"Papa." It was Penelope's voice. "Papa, what is happening?"

"I am not sure, Penelope . . . Sarah is in contact with you, yes?"

"Yes, she is very strong . . . I cannot fight her . . . I am very tired."

Penelope looked up at the rest of us. "KC . . . Air? You are here too?"

"Dr. Dredalus," I shouted, "Penelope's free of Sarah Jane . . . Let's get her out of here while we can.

"No!" said that same disembodied voice, then Penelope's body went rigid again just as Dr. Dredalus was about to reach for her. "Elliot," said the voice, "You . . . must . . . tell . . . me!"

Now Mr. Foote was frantic. "Sarah Jane! Tell you *what* . . . ? I didn't have anything to do with what happened . . . I had nothing to do with Billy McDuff and his friends. I didn't help them trick you into coming down here. You must believe me! I swear it!"

"No, Elliot! You . . . must . . . tell . . . it! Tell . . . your . . . deep . . . dark . . . secret!"

Mr. Foote turned to us. "I don't know what she's talking about. It was so long ago."

I turned to Air. "This isn't getting us anywhere! We've got to do something! As long as Penelope and Brett are down there, Sarah Jane has exactly where she wants us."

"KC, dude, what can we do?"

"Let's go down there and bring Penelope and Brett to the shallow end of the pool and bring them up. I think we have to get Penelope as far from Sarah Jane as we can . . . And stop calling me *dude*! Come on!"

As we ran along the edge of the pool, Dr. Dredalus shouted, "What are you kids doing? Stop, you'll ruin everything, *stop!*"

There was just enough light for Air and me to find our way to the other end of the Olympic-size pool. We jumped down into the empty pool at the three-foot level. The whole room was like a huge dark cavern. At the opposite end, I could see Dr. Dredalus, Penelope, and Brett all bathed in the soft gray-green light.

I turned to Air. "I really don't have a plan . . ."

"We could rush her."

"That sounds like a plan . . . Let's *go!*"

We sprinted toward them, trying to rush Penelope and take Sarah Jane by surprise. We were only fifteen or so feet from Penelope when she whirled around and thrust out her arms. Air and I were knocked back. We landed hard on the pool floor.

"Ouch, man. This is worse than doing a stalefish off oncoming traffic. You okay, KC?"

I was crouched, ready to try again. "I'm good, but ghost or not, this girl is really starting to tick me off!"

"Whoa, chill. That's still Penny there."

"I know! Come on, one more rush at her . . . This time, from different sides!"

"Man, I wish I had my skate gear . . . This is gonna be some serious hurtage!"

"GO!" I sprinted as fast as I could at Penelope. Air was a heartbeat behind me. My big plan was to tackle Penelope, maybe shake Sarah Jane's grip on her, and then get her out of pool. But Sarah Jane wasn't having any part of it. Air and I came up hard against something, like a wall we couldn't see.

I was back on the pool floor, looking at Penelope. She was just standing there with a really mad look on her face. Behind her, Dr. Dredalus was looking on with a really scared expression on his face.

"KC, you and the young man must stop . . . This is not helping."

Judging from the expression of Penelope's face, he was right. The glow surrounding her intensified, turning from a gray-green to a ghastly orange, and Penelope looked as if she was in a wind tunnel. Her hair and clothes were whipping around her. There was the sound of metal twisting and huge pipes creaking behind the walls of the pool. Suddenly there was an explosion of the rustiest, foulest water I've ever seen.

"She's flooding the pool! Both of you, out now!" shouted Penelope's dad as he fought his way toward his daughter and Brett Henry. But Sarah Jane resisted, sending Dr. Dredalus back and up the ladder.

"He stays!" shouted the possessed Penelope, pointing at Brett, who was sitting up but obviously still groggy. By the time Air and I fought our way through the torrent to another ladder, the water was already up to our ankles. We climbed up, and I sloshed over to Mr. Foote and Penelope's dad. "Mr. Foote . . . you've got to think! She said something about a deep, dark secret. Come on. They're going to drown if you don't do something fast!"

Mr. Foote held his head in his hands. Then he staggered over to the ladder and sagged against it. Below him, Brett was still sitting on the floor, now fully awake. The water was up to his chest.

"Uncle Elliot," he screamed above the roar of the water, "help me! I can't get up! Something's holding me down!"

"Sarah Jane . . . let him go!" Mr. Foote pleaded. "He didn't do anything to you!"

"Elliot!" said Penelope. "tell me your secret! The deep dark secret!" Suddenly she lurched as if something violently yanked her. Then a gray mist seemed to pour out of Penelope, forming something above her. It was a figure of a girl. Her face twisted in rage. Waves of angry orange light streamed from the apparition.

"Look!" I yelled. "That was what I saw in Mr. Foote's office. It's . . . Sarah Jane."

"Yes, yes . . . ," said Dr. Dredalus. "She's manifested herself . . . But now she's no longer in full possession of Penelope."

A look of understanding crossed Penelope's face. "Mr. Foote . . . there is something Sarah Jane must hear from you . . . She thinks that you had something to do with the prank that led to the accident . . . something about a letter you wrote. She is so angry and sad. She thought that you were friends." Then she slumped. Brett Henry stood up just in time to catch her before she went under the waist-high water. "Mr. Foote . . . you had a secret that you wanted to tell her that night," she said weakly. "Something important, but something you kept to yourself. Something the others found out about that they used to lure her into this room."

"I had nothing to do with them. What they did to Sarah was cruel . . . unforgivable . . . Wait." Then Mr. Foote placed his hands over his mouth in shock. He slumped even more against the ladder. "There was a note I had written to Sarah's best friend, Agnes Perault. Yes, that has to be it! I remember writing to Agnes that I had a secret to tell Sarah Jane."

"Please, Mr. Foote," said Penelope, "if you remember anything, please tell her. Call her by name and tell *her!*"

"Sarah Jane . . . yes, I wrote a note to Agnes asking her to please try to convince you to be at the dance that night. It was so important back then. Sarah, you were so smart and funny, and I liked being around you so much. I wanted to ask you to *go steady*. That was my only secret. I was so shy . . . I kept my feelings in through most of high school. I finally worked up the nerve to ask you. But I never had anything to do with McDuff and his friends. Somehow, they must have found out about my asking you to go steady. They must have used it to play their trick. We were always so serious as students. They always made fun of us. Played gags on us. Oh, Sarah Jane, I'm so sorry this happened to you . . . I'm so sorry things didn't turn out differently."

Penelope moaned, and she seemed to collapse against Brett Henry. Above them, the apparition had already started to fade. But the fading glow of what had been Sarah Jane McCormack was now a pale, peaceful blue. Just before she faded away, I thought I saw a faint sad smile on her face.

We all stood there for several minutes stunned by what we had just seen. Dr. Dredalus gently tried to revive his daughter. Then there was suddenly a commotion above us. A dozen or more firefighters and medical technicians were crowded around the gaping hole in the ceiling, looking down at us.

BOB BERRY

Chapter 19

Rescued

I DON'T KNOW what the emergency personnel were thinking as they took us out of Richelieu High School that night. They carried Mr. Foote, Brett Henry, and Penelope out on stretchers. They were all placed into ambulances. Penelope's dad stayed by her side. They took Air and me up to another ambulance and asked us if we were hurt. We were probably bruised more than anyone else, but we were still standing. They looked us over and released us to our parents who were waiting with the huge crowd that had assembled outside the school. I guess news had spread that there was an accident at the school. A lot of terrified families rushed to the school. I won't go into details about how my mom and dad reacted when they saw me, but trust me. It was major drama!

The following day, there were reporters at our door. Mr. Cortez had asked that we not speak to them until he and the authorities had interviewed us. So we spent most of Saturday peering out of our windows and keeping a low profile. I was exhausted and slept late.

That night, I called Penelope's house, but I only got the answering machine. I tried her cell, nada. No response to my e-mail either. My dad guessed that she was probably still in the hospital.

Sunday morning, I came down to breakfast and was bummed to find Mr. Cortez and some other school district officials sitting in our living room, "chatting" over coffee with my parents.

"You see our problem, Mr. and Mrs. Watson, we firmly believe a story like this in the media could have a terrible result for our students. There would surely be an army of media at our school, interviewing the student body in general and your daughter in particular. I'm sure none of us want that kind of exposure for our children or our school."

"That's going to be a pretty hard story to suppress, isn't it?" asked Dad.

"Your daughter, Alonzo Rodriguez, Dr. Dredalus and Penelope, the Henry boy, and Mr. Foote were the only ones actually remaining in the building at the time of the floor collapse. Everyone else had fled when the power went down. I understand that it was quite a stampede. Fortunately, no one was hurt."

"And how do you explain that they were in the basement when you found them?" asked Mom.

"All we know is that Brett Henry and Ms. Dredalus did fall through the floor. Fortunately, the hole was over the deep end of the pool, which was nearly full at the time due to the rupture of a water main. The others went down the basement to effect a rescue. All very coincidental, but believable. That is the official story."

"But, Mr. Cortez," I blurted out, "that's not true! The pool wasn't filled, and Penelope and Brett floated down to the basement."

"Ms. Watson . . . KC, please try to see this from our perspective. As unbelievable as it is, your version of the events of Friday night will be an invitation to exploitive journalists and paranormal loonies. The school will be overrun with kooks and amateur ghost hunters. We might as well close down the school. I've spoken with Dr. Dredalus, and as a professional in these matters, he agrees on this course."

Dad sat back. "Well, Mr. Cortez, I guess it's the only logical thing to do . . . Frankly, I've got my doubts about the whole thing. It all sounds like some kind of mass hysteria. But I, for one, don't want to live in the middle of a media circus. What do we need to do now?"

One of the officials, a woman in a gray business suit, produced a thick document from her briefcase. All you need to do is sign this confidentiality agreement. It's legally binding. It promises the school that you will refuse to talk to any media about this affair and that you will not publish any books or articles about this episode." I was shocked when Dad signed. I was crushed; my dad didn't believe me or anything that had happened. I just stood there staring at the floor.

They all shook hands and left. I went up to my room to put the beat down on my pillow.

Later that day, I asked my parents if they could drive me to the hospital. I wanted to see Penelope. Thankfully, they agreed without too much argument. When we got there, Dr. Dredalus and Gustave were sitting in a resting area, drinking coffee and reading dog-eared magazines. I introduced my parents and my little brother to them.

"Penelope has been asleep, but I'm sure she is awake now. She has been asking for you. Come. I'll walk you to her room."

My folks sat down, looking a little awkward. James busied himself with his Nintendo.

Once we were out of earshot, Dr. Dredalus turned toward me. "KC, I must thank you personally for standing by my daughter. We have moved so many times. Having a friend like you means the world to her. And to me . . . Thank you." He bowed slightly and grasped my hand then gently ushered me into Penelope's room. He remained outside.

When I walked into her room, she was lying in the hospital bed, watching some lame reality show on TV. They had her hooked up to an IV, and there was some glowing thing on her index finger. She smiled weakly when she saw me. I couldn't help myself, and I ran over and hugged her. She looked a lot better than two nights ago. Her color was back; her eyes were back to their tawny cat color. Her hair was a bit of a mess, and sometime in the past forty-eight hours, the hair at her temples had turned a stark white.

"Like the new hairstyle?" she asked. "I understand that it is from shock."

"I guess it looks cool . . . Now you look more *goth* than ever."

"More like Penny Dreadful, yes?" Then she laughed.

"Hey, that's not my nickname for you. That was Air's!"

"I know. Maybe it fits. How is Air? I think he took quite a few falls that night."

"He did." Then I felt a twinge in my stomach as I realized that I had never called him.

"He'll understand."

"What . . . ? Hey, how did you know I was thinking about Air?"

"You haven't guessed by now? I'm sensitive . . . I can read people, their emotions, sometimes their thoughts. This is why I am so active in my father's investigations. My mother was the same way."

"You must really miss her."

"I do, more than you can know . . . But she has not passed away. She just *isn't here* now." Then she became very quiet.

Changing the subject, I said, "Sooo you're a psychic, huh? How cool is that?"

"We don't use that term. I'm sensitive."

"Okay, and don't you think that you should have given me the 411? Wasn't that vital information? Maybe I would have picked up on Sarah Jane possessing you earlier." There I was, getting mad at her again. But she grabbed my hand and looked at me.

"KC, I'm sorry. Usually I've found that it is better just to hide it. People act so weird when they know."

"Yeah, I guess I understand. So when do you get out of here? You must be going bonkers."

"I would like to leave today, but my father says that I can go home tomorrow . . . I am still *under observation*."

I felt a little uncomfortable suddenly. I guess the fact that she could read me so well was starting to make me feel weird. "Y'know, you're right to keeping this whole sensitivity thing on the QT . . . It does make people feel a little uneasy."

"KC, I promise I'll never try to read you . . . And besides, you've taught me that what a friend does is more important than what a friend says . . . or thinks. I'm not reading your mind now . . . But you do have to call Air and find out how he is . . . Tell him I was asking for him."

We hugged again, and I left her room. I was a little sad to leave her alone. I turned around to see her dad and Gustave enter her room. Whatever the deal was with her mother, I was glad she had them.

When I got home, I called Air.

"Hey."

"KC! Whoa! I know I should've called, but my mom said I should let you rest. How are you?"

"I'm good. How about you?"

"Totally awesome! That was the sickest night of my life. Got some real gnarly boos, but I'm okay. Ghost hunting makes boarding look like a walk in the park."

"Wow . . . Sounds like you're stoked."

"Totally. Too bad we can't tell anyone about it."

"I guess you got the visit from Cortez and the rest of the suits . . . ?"

"Yup, bright and early."

"Look, maybe we can get together later . . . I mean, I know it's getting late and tomorrow's school, but I'd like to see you."

"Sure, KC. Just give me the when and where."

"Battle Park in about five minutes . . . I'll take Frisket for a walk."

"I'm there. See you in five."

Five minutes later, Air was kicking his skateboard down Whitney. When he came to the curb, he did a perfect heel flip, landing the board and himself on the sidewalk.

"Nice!"

"Thanks. Suddenly I'm boarding better than ever. I guess I just needed to shake things up a bit."

"Maybe adventure and excitement appeals to you."

"I guess."

"Listen, Air, uh, Alonzo, I just wanted to thank you. You saved my life."

"No sweat, KC. That's what friends are for . . ."

"Exactly. But still, thanks. And thanks for taking the rest of the ride . . . I'm not sure we helped that much, but it all ended okay."

"Except we can never tell anyone about what happened. Who'd believe it anyway?"

"You never know. Somebody might. I kept a journal on everything that happened, all the way back to the first day of school."

"No way."

"Way."

"Am I in it?"

"Dude, you're one of the heroes."

"No way!"

"Way!"

Chapter 20

FYI

IT WAS NEARLY Thanksgiving by the time I finally finished writing down everything that had happened over the last couple of months. Since Halloween, things really settled down, and I got back to concentrating on schoolwork and all the social activities that high school offered. Air and Penelope and I have gone to a few school dances together. They were fun although they had to be held in the cafeteria while the gym was being repaired. Brett Henry even asked Penelope to dance a couple of times. I think that he might actually like her a little. Turned out that Penelope almost broke his arm the night of the Halloween dance, and in some weird jock way, that really got her some serious props. So now a lot of the jocks were asking her out. *Go figure.*

Since the gym had been under reconstruction, PE classes had been held outside or sometimes early in the day in the cafeteria. Mr. Foote told Penelope and me that he was going to retire before the New Year. He told us that after Sarah Jane's accident, he always felt that he had to stay around the school. Penelope thinks that unconsciously, he knew that he still had unfinished business with Sarah Jane.

Speaking about unfinished business, one day Penelope handed me an old brittle note scrawled on yellowed blue-lined notebook paper. I unfolded it carefully and was floored to see that it was the note that Mr. Foote had written to Agnes Perault fifty years ago. You know, the one with the "deep, dark, secret." It turned out that Mrs. Perault was the one who let the popular kids know that Mr. Foote was going to ask Sarah Jane to go steady. She hadn't done it to be mean or anything. She was just excited about her friends getting together and told the wrong girl. That was how they were able to get Sarah Jane down into the basement. Poor Mrs. Perault was carrying the guilt around all these years.

I was sad because Penelope told me that she would be in Greece over the Christmas holiday. That was a bummer. She would be on some kind of investigation with her dad. But she promised to bring me back something really cool. I couldn't wait. The day she left, I found a tiny package on the bench on our front porch. It was addressed to me in her handwriting.

Dear KC,

When my father brought me back to our home on Whitney Street, I had mixed feelings about being here again. I was born in White Plains and spent my first four years living at 333 Whitney Street. The house has many memories of those days, particularly of my mother. This is a little trinket she hung on my bedroom window. It is a dream catcher, and it is very dear to me. It is made by the Native Americans to catch their nightmares. Because you have been such a wonderful friend, I'm asking you to keep this until I return. I guarantee you will sleep well with this dream catcher guarding you. Until the New Year.

Love,
Penelope (a.k.a Penny Dreadful, ha ha) :)

After reading the note, I couldn't help getting a little teary. Penelope could really get under my skin, but without her here, things just weren't as exciting. The best present she can get me is just to come back home.

Edwards Brothers,Inc!
Thorofare, NJ 08086
09 July, 2010
BA2010190